MAGGIE CASPER

NIGHTS

Includes the Novels: Zane's Way and Honoring Sean

ELLORA'S CAVE
ROMANTICA PUBLISHING

What the critics are saying...

ଚ୍ଚ

Zane's Way

"(Zane's Way) is incredibly erotic and a touching love story. [...] Zane's Way is the only way." ~ *Love Romances*

"The first book in the O'Malley Wild trilogy, Zane's Way starts things off with a bang... Both erotic and emotional, Zane's Way is not to be missed." ~ *Romance Reviews Today*

4 Angels "Funny, sensational and passionate are a few words used to describe Zane's Way by Maggie Casper. [...] This is a terrific novel for anyone who takes pleasure in reading a magnificent BDSM story." ~ *Fallen Angel Reviews*

4 Stars "The sexual tension is exquisite throughout this entire story. Zane and Serena's journey to a closer, happier union is realistic and touching. It's also unbelievably hot. I definitely recommend this book." ~ *Just Erotic Romance Reviews*

Honoring Sean

5 Angels "Maggie Casper has written an unforgettable story that you will not be able to put doen." ~ *Fallen Angel Reviews*

5 Cups "This is a wonderful story. [...] A must read." ~ *Coffee Time Romance*

An Ellora's Cave Romantica Publication

www.ellorascave.com

Naughty Nights

ISBN 9781419954979
ALL RIGHTS RESERVED.
Zane's Way Copyright © 2004 Maggie Casper
Honoring Sean Copyright © 2005 Maggie Casper
Edited by Mary Moran.
Cover art by Syneca.

This book printed in the U.S.A. by Jasmine–Jade Enterprises, LLC.

Trade paperback publication March 2006

Also by Maggie Casper

ಐ

Christmas Cash
Maverick's Black Cat
O'Malley Wild: Hayden's Hellion
O'Malley Wild: Tying the Knot

About the Author

ಐ

Maggie Casper's life could be called many things but boring isn't one of them. If asked, Maggie would tell you that blessed would more aptly describe her everyday existence.

Being loved by four gorgeous daughters should be enough to make anybody feel blessed. Add to that a bit of challenge, a lot of fun and an undeniably close circle of friends and family and you'd be walking in her shoes.

A love of reading was passed on by Maggie's mother at a very early age, and so began her addiction to romance novels. Maggie admits to writing some in high school but when life got in the way, she put her pen and paper up. Seems that things changed over the years because when she finally decided it was time to put her story ideas on paper, the pen was out and the computer was in. Took her a while to catch up but she finally made it.

When not writing, Maggie can usually be found reading, doing genealogy research or watching NASCAR.

Maggie welcomes comments from readers. You can find her website and email address on her author bio page at www.ellorascave.com.

Tell Us What You Think

We appreciate hearing reader opinions about our books. You can email us at Comments@EllorasCave.com.

NAUGHTY NIGHTS

O'Malley Wild

ଛ

ZANE'S WAY

Dedication

એ

Thank you to R.H. whose wonderful song gave me the idea for Zane's Way, the title that started the series.

This book is dedicated to my daughters, who remind me daily of what is important with as little as a brilliant smile.

Between the four of you, you manage to brighten even the darkest of days. Always keep your chins up, stay strong and when times call for it, be tough.

Thank you for being you. I love you!

Trademarks Acknowledgement

એ

The author acknowledges the trademarked status and trademark owners of the following wordmarks mentioned in this work of fiction:

Stetson: John B. Stetson Company

Wrangler: Wrangler Apparel Corp.

Prologue

A grunt of completion filled the air rising above their heavy breaths. Rena fought to bury the feelings of inadequacy as Zane rolled away, his broad shoulders now facing her. Before her heart had time to resume its normal pace, the TV was turned on, its dim light flickering around her, intensifying the feelings tearing at her heart.

She distractedly smoothed her hand across the sheet trying to absorb its warmth. Her body shivered in response to the loss of heat.

Her insides mourned the loss. *You should feel blessed*, her mind scolded. And yet, she didn't. Being in a long-term relationship should bring a feeling of contentment, but for Serena Keller the only thing it brought, at least when it came to her sex life, was a heavy ache that reminded her daily of what was missing.

"Zane," she called softly.

The only answer from his side of the bed was a grumpy rumble. Not allowing that to dissuade her, Serena asked, "Did I satisfy you? Was it good?"

"Why do you ask that?" It was obvious he was annoyed, but why? She tried to keep her voice calm when she answered.

"Just wondered…" she finally said, her voice trailing off.

"You're always wondering things, Rena. Just let it be."

She didn't say anything—just lay there, thinking to herself.

So many times in the past year, she had silently fought with herself. How could she possibly fix the problem? In every other way, her relationship was one to be envied. The fact she lived week after week, month after month through monotonous sex shouldn't really matter. Right? Wrong! Her body screamed as it craved more. So much more.

Staring at the ceiling, she thought about the man next to her. His body wide and warm as his arms welcomed her. Why wasn't it enough?

So often, she witnessed his hooded eyes following her as she moved about their home. The way they traveled over each inch of her as if remembering every freckle, every crease. Just thinking of it made her shiver. Often she could feel the vibes coming off him in waves. The only way to describe the vibes he bestowed upon her was molten. So hot, she felt as if the areas his gaze raked would be singed.

There was a sense of unbridled passion lying just below the surface. Although he never ever lost control there had been several times she'd backed down from a heated argument due to a specific look his eyes took when he was close to the edge. The way he narrowed them when mad. Even angry, he kept himself together.

Serena often wondered what would happen if she gave that extra little push. As a child, her smart mouth and sassy attitude had gotten her into her share of trouble. As an adult, she learned to choose her battles wisely, to control herself. She often wondered if the fierce control she held over herself these days was a protective mechanism. A way to help prevent the past from intruding.

A hoot made her jump, reminding her she wasn't alone. The football game blared through the speakers as her body fought its lingering need. Although an assertive woman, Serena often wished she could be more aggressive. She could only remember a handful of times over the past four years that she had initiated sex. Even though she knew her lack of confidence was part of the problem, she just couldn't bring herself to do it, to initiate intimacy between the two of them. So much had taken place in her youth leaving impressions she longed to forget. She knew she couldn't because they were so deeply integrated into who she was. A person she hoped to change.

The tips of her fingers tingled with the need to stroke the tanned skin of his shoulders. To caress him with her hands while her mouth attacked his, her teeth nipping at his full lower lip. Why couldn't she give in?

Over the past year, she had begun to look deeply inside herself. To find the things she wanted to change, things that were very hard to admit, even to herself. The fact she wanted to be dominated in the bedroom had come as an utter shock. It had been hard enough to admit it to herself, but how did you go about admitting it to another?

It was mind-boggling that she would crave the precise thing that had ended her marriage.

Even during the best of times, the horrible memories came flooding back. Serena ran a shaky hand along her throat, then through the tangles of her hair. She would not think about it.

Would things be different this time? She wasn't sure, but even if she thought they would be she just couldn't bring herself to the point of making her desires known. The though of disappointing Zane scared her. If she admitted her needs, would he think she was twisted? Would he want her less?

The pessimistic thoughts brought a frown to her face, but in the semi-darkness of the bedroom, there was no one to see it.

It was as if she were stuck between a rock and a hard spot. If she said nothing, things would never change. Could she go on forever wondering "what if"?

Her life was simple. Kept busy by a job she loved and a deep fondness for Zane. Those two things kept her comfortable. Of course, that was another part of the problem—she no longer wanted things to merely be comfortable.

The thought of being a bit uncomfortable, of feeling the generous length of Zane's shaft as it tunneled with fierce thrusts through her sopping center was what she wanted. It was what her body was all but demanding.

She needed for Zane to treat her as a woman, a woman whose body was made for loving. Not as a hothouse flower, touching her as if she was delicate glass.

The fact they had always gotten along well together both in the bedroom and out was comforting, but had there ever been that spark? The one talked about over and over in the erotic romance books she devoured.

Feelings ran deep, but Serena could not remember a time where they had let loose resulting in hot, sweaty sex.

How could she forget everything she'd been taught in the past and just go for it?

Would she be able to explain that more times than not, her sexual fantasies consisted of bondage? Sex where she was utterly dominated and brought so much pleasure she thought she would expire from the sheer force of it.

Could she explain to the man lying next to her that sometimes a woman wanted to be fucked instead of loved? She gave an unladylike snort at the thought. Shaking her head, she brought herself back into the present. There was no way she would ever in a million years be able to tell Zane what she longed for.

Back to square one and feeling a bit down in the dumps about the whole thing, Serena swung her legs off the edge of the bed and padded silently down the hall. Ice cream would make her feel better. There was nothing like double chocolate chip to solve the sexual problems of women everywhere.

* * * * *

Zane O'Malley felt like a man possessed. Watching the gentle sway of Rena's hips as she walked down the hall brought his semi-erect cock to attention. The curve of her ass as it met the uppermost part of her thighs was one of his favorite parts of her body.

There was just something about her that had his libido engaged in a constant battle. If that wasn't the damnedest thing, he didn't know what was. Over the years of their relationship, he had learned to keep a tight rein on his lustful thoughts. Afraid that if he let loose, she would pull away from him and they would never have a chance to see where their relationship would end up.

Sometimes it was harder than others, but so far, he'd managed to control himself. Moving halfway across the United States was the only thing that kept the knowledge of his past from Serena. He often wondered what would happen if they ran into an old flame or one of his brothers. How would she take the news that he was not the man she thought him to be? The news that he liked his women submissive and ready.

He thought of packing up and moving home in order to be closer to his family, but had yet to bring it up in conversation. What would her reaction be if she were to find out just how much he had been holding back over the past four years? Knowing about her past helped keep him in control, but it was getting harder and harder to keep the animal at bay. Something was going to have to give, and soon.

His feelings for Rena were genuine, he would never intentionally hurt her, but he felt trapped, unfulfilled. Like a caged animal willing to do anything for release. It took every ounce of willpower to let her go every morning when what he really longed to do was to fuck her into oblivion. He often thought of taking her aggressively, or rubbing his cock between the cheeks of her ass before breaching the tight passage.

The messages drummed into his head throughout childhood kept him from treating her in a way she might find offensive when what he really wanted to do was take her in every position possible while she was bound and blindfolded.

He would then release his pent-up fantasies by pounding into her tight sheath with every inch of his rock-hard cock. She would cry and beg for it and in the moment her ever-explosive body found its release and satisfaction, she would shudder through one orgasm after another until he was sure she was thoroughly drained.

At that time, he would come deep within her. Keeping himself buried to the hilt, allowing no separation throughout the night, forcing his length deep every time she tried to move. Keeping her body hostage, at the same time imprisoning his within her.

Breaking through her controlled exterior was a goal, almost an obsession if the truth were told. If he had his way, there would be no more quiet lovemaking. Tiny moans and muffled gasps were not enough when what he longed to hear were screams. Begging, pleading and pleasure-induced sobs telling of the sweet torture her body could no longer resist.

Instead, he treated Rena as if she might break. Sometimes he wondered what would happen if he pushed. If instead of giving her the choice, he took her the way his body ached to, hard, deep and fast.

Would she balk if he insisted she submit to him in every way where sex was concerned? Would she leave if he pressed? So many questions and no damned answers! It was extremely frustrating.

Every nerve in his body tingled at the thought of his Rena blindfolded, hands cuffed high over head while he worked her over until she could no longer remain the quiet, controlled woman she struggled to be.

He had taken to doing something, anything as soon as they were finished with sex in order not to push her. From there, things went downhill. It was almost to the point of penciling in a time and date for intercourse.

To make matters worse, they seemed to only have sex in the dark and never got very inventive when it came to positions or exploring. Boring sex was almost as bad as no sex. Well, not quite, but close.

A lot of the blame could be pinned on him, he would be the first to admit. They were stuck in a rut and it seemed neither did a thing to change it. He didn't press and she didn't offer. It was comfortable.

He realized a short time ago that they were probably still together because it was easier to stay together than it was to split up. Thinking of it that way grated on his nerves, but it was the truth.

The thought of having a fling had crossed his mind on many occasions, but as of yet he hadn't been able to bring himself to do it. Without assessing his feelings for Rena too closely, he just didn't feel right about it. And yet, his body yearned to feel the power coursing through it as had happened when he'd been a single man bedding a submissive woman.

The excitement and control was unlike anything else he could think to compare it to. Giving that up for the past four years had turned him into a different man, one he wasn't sure he liked much. The outgoing Zane O'Malley was gone. He'd been replaced by an uptight, nine-to-five, three-piece suit. It was time some changes were made. He just needed to figure out how to go about doing it without hurting himself or Rena in the process.

No longer willing to dwell upon an unpredictable future, Zane left the warmth of the comforter covering him and went to see where Rena was.

He found her standing at the kitchen counter, foot tapping in time to classic rock softly sounding from the speakers. It made him hurt. His body always seemed to go on alert where his sassy lover was concerned. Her pink tongue kept darting out to lick ice cream from a cone. His shaft pulsed with every flick of her tasting tongue.

He could picture the same pink tongue licking him. With his eyes closed, he could almost feel each lick she bestowed upon the creamy confection.

If only he could do what his body hungered to do. Only the thought of alienating her stopped him. Instead he did what he knew would keep him on track. He started a conversation having nothing to do with their physical relationship.

"So, have you heard anything from your new clients?" he asked trying to focus on anything besides the way she lapped at the ice cream cone.

Serena whirled around, upending her cone in the process. The ice cream fell top down with a splat onto the floor.

"Sorry," he said watching as she moved silently back to the counter where she retrieved a wad of paper towels.

"That's okay," she said as she bent to clean the sticky mess. She then leaned over giving him a peck on the cheek. "I have a meeting with the business owners tomorrow, so I won't know anything until then."

He knew Rena loved her job and she was good at it. Making personal and business websites kept her busy and it was a job she could perform from home. "Is it a personal or business website they want to hire you for?" he asked conversationally.

"I really don't know," she said. Nose scrunched, she shook her head. "They were sort of secretive in their e-mail to me. It said they preferred to meet me in person to speak about the details. I don't even know what type of site I'm being hired to build."

Her face remained scrunched up. It was a look he loved. One reminding him of a disgruntled Kewpie doll.

Zane thought it over for a minute before he cautioned her.

"Be careful, baby. Don't go anywhere alone with them."

Rena assured him she would be meeting her prospective clients in a public place at lunchtime so there would be nothing to worry about.

With that, he gave her a slow gentle kiss just the way he always did before going to bed, then left the kitchen.

It was quite a while before Rena joined him. Where had she been? What was she doing? He could picture her sitting in front of her computer, staring at the screen with her green eyes glazed in concentration.

Did she think about their lack of sex or the fact their sex life was as boring as a Mr. Rogers rerun? Probably not, he thought with a half smile.

If everything his mother had taught him about women was true then Rena more than likely never gave sex more than a passing thought. He wondered how women could be so different. His mother, a true gentle woman warned him of his overbearing bedroom manners after hearing stories of his sexcapades. It probably didn't help any that he had been caught in the act on one occasion.

He still grimaced every time he remembered the look on her face at that very moment. To find him plowing the prom queen right there on the living room couch probably hadn't been the highlight of her life either.

She had repeatedly scolded him for treating women improperly. So often, she tried to make him believe that any woman who liked the dark, lustier side of sex was deranged. He still laughed at the thought, but felt the need to heed her teachings when it came to Serena Keller. Her slight build and milky-white complexion brought out the protective side of him. Even if it was someone like him she needed to be protected from.

He watched from beneath lowered lashes as Serena slipped silently into the room and climbed back into bed. Within moments, she was asleep. The deep even breaths coming from the woman beside him were relaxing.

He snuggled up close behind her, his mind wandering back to a time before Rena. A time when his body insisted on taking what it needed from the women he brought to his bed. He could no longer remember names or even faces—only the explosive coupling remained with him.

He missed the wild abandon. The difference was that the other women had known about the O'Malley brothers. They went into the relationships, no matter how short-lived, knowing exactly what to expect.

That wasn't the case with Rena. She grew up pretty much alone. Marrying young had not been a good experience for her, leaving her unsure and wary about men. He never wanted her to feel the shame and humiliation she'd felt while in the arms of her ex-husband.

Memories assailed him. He wanted to wrap his hands around the throat of the bastard who dared to treat Rena like a slab of meat. That night so long ago, when she'd bared her soul, unburdening her heart, had left him shaken. Had his unusual sexual tastes ever left a woman feeling the same? Thinking back, he was sure that wasn't the case. He might have loved being dominant when it came to sex, but all present had been willing and eager.

Pleasing a woman, hearing the sultry words spill from her lips as he pushed her over the edge, that's what got him off.

Such thoughts kept him awake until finally his eyes grew heavy, then the dreams took over. Dreams of bondage and total capitulation with a woman he loved. Exciting sex that kept both parties teetering on the edge. Did such a thing exist? It must, his sleep-drugged brain taunted him. It's just a matter of finding and training the right woman.

Chapter One
&

Serena checked her appearance one last time in the mirrored closet door. The hug of her navy blue skirt was neither too tight nor too loose. As always, her attire was completely professional. The white silk shirt never dipped too low, a button never left undone. She often wondered how the woman staring back at her could be so outwardly different from the one buried deep inside.

Nylon-clad feet slipped easily into comfortable pumps. Tiny gold studs graced her ears, the only jewelry except her watch to adorn her body. A pink-tipped finger ran the length of her collarbone moving inward until it reached the dip at the base of her throat.

Her green eyes watched the movement in the mirror. Never once, as her fingers slid smoothly over her skin, did she long for a shiny gold necklace. No, her taste ran more toward the exotic, a collar. One, that would show ownership of her body. A body longing to be lovingly possessed.

It was hard to get used to. The fact she was no longer the conservative woman she strived to be. The exact moment things began to change couldn't be pinpointed. It was like a slow transformation, one she wasn't sure would ever be complete. That may very well be what frightened her most, the fact that she had no time limit to follow. It was like being left dangling on the end of a rope. A very precarious feeling for a woman who insisted on always being in control.

Control and the need to always feel it was what disturbed her. It was okay in her everyday life but no longer worked for her private life. How would she ever learn to experiment, to experience, if she couldn't give up the control she held so tightly?

And yet, if she did give up control of her body, of her sexuality, would she lose herself in the process? Too many questions and not enough answers. It was so frustrating to need so deeply and not know how to go about finding a means to satisfy that need.

"Good luck with your meeting, Rena. You'll knock their socks off, I'm sure." The way he came up behind her all quiet and controlled startled her. She'd been so engrossed with her inner thoughts that she'd missed him in the mirror as he'd come up behind her.

"Thank you," she whispered as he leaned in and kissed the side of her neck just below her ear. "I'll call you when I'm finished," she added when normal brain function returned. Her neck still felt warm and tingly from his kiss and the feathering of his breath across her skin, as he talked low and husky near her ear.

Serena listened intently as he once again cautioned her, reminding her to stay in the restaurant and to call if she needed him for anything.

When he left for work, she couldn't help but wonder what her relationship with Zane would be like had they started out communicating instead of just letting things happen. Would things have evolved into a more open relationship? Would they be having knee-buckling sex on a nightly basis? Under those circumstances, would she have been able to tell him of all her secret fantasies without the inner turmoil she now felt?

There has to be something I can do, she thought as she made her way into the kitchen to retrieve her purse. Some way to get what she longed for, what her body, mind and soul craved without being unfaithful. Could she find a way? And if so, how would she know it was the right decision?

The twenty-minute drive to the restaurant left her a lot of time to think. What exactly was it she was looking for? There were so many sides to eroticism. She had to be sure of her wants and needs before she could even begin to make plans. And yet how could she be sure without any experience?

Domination. Bondage. Loss of control. These were among the things her mind mentally checked off. To be able to have a loving trusting relationship with a man who would leave her no choice. Those thoughts alone were enough to make her skin tingle, the flesh of her inner thighs heat causing her to become slick with her own juices.

Damn! Good thing she'd taken to carrying extra panties in her bag. Erotically sensual thoughts seemed to keep her aroused and wet.

Hell, the way things had been going lately she might be better off to forego panties altogether.

Would she be able to find a man who could take her in hand and teach her submission without humiliation? The thought of being degraded or hurt was not at all appealing. A little pain could go a long way, so how could she know for sure what a partner might do?

She couldn't, that was part of the excitement. The fear factor. Fear of the unknown—of letting go.

Pulling into the large parking lot, Serena took one last look in her rearview mirror to be sure no wisps of hair had escaped the tight twist at the nape of her neck. Probably one more thing on the long list of things she could control.

Upon entering the restaurant, Serena was met by a hostess.

"May I help you, ma'am?" the neatly dressed woman asked.

"Serena Keller. I'm meeting the Bennetts," Serena answered politely nodding her thanks when the woman motioned her to follow.

Immediately, she was whisked away into the dimly lit interior. With chin lifted and back straight, she followed the woman through the cozily furnished room. The whole time her eyes were riveted on a couple sitting closely together at a table in the far corner.

The voluptuous brunette was smiling into the face of a handsome man with hair the color of sand. He idly stroked the back of her hand where it rested on the tabletop.

He looked as if he might devour her on the spot. She looked like a woman who would willingly climb onto the center of the table and let him have his way right there for all to see. There was no discomfort, no unease in their movements.

It was a brief second before Serena realized she'd been led to and stood staring at the very couple she'd excitedly watched on her journey across the room.

Moving as one, the couple stood. Glad for a tiny respite, she gave her drink order to an eager waiter. Fighting her embarrassment at being caught staring, Serena stuck out a hand.

"Hello," she said. "I'm Serena Keller."

The handsome man standing across from her took her hand in his. "Nice to meet you, Ms Keller." His palm was warm and his firm grasp sent a jolt of awareness straight up her arm. This man may seem relaxed and carefree, but nothing could be farther from the truth. Continuing, he said. "I'm Josh Bennett and this is Jenna."

"Please, call me Serena." She wasn't quite sure, but something about this couple was different. The difference might be subtle, but it was there.

"Okay, Serena," he said as he released her hand.

Serena shifted her gaze to the woman standing beside him. She was of average height, but that's where anything average about her stopped. Exotic almond-shaped eyes stared back. Golden flawless skin covered perfect bone structure and her body was to die for. She had yet to speak.

Josh leaned in and whispered something in her ear, making the woman smile. A blush crept from her chest to her neck then higher. Serena could tell the woman wore no bra. Pierced nipples stood proudly erect against the peach shirt highlighting her golden tan. The neckline was square and low. Collarbones thrust out above full breasts.

That's when she noticed it, the collar. It wasn't a necklace, not in the sense of what she considered normal. Wide and fitted, it was an intricate work of gold and about the sexiest thing she'd ever seen.

The woman introduced to her as Jenna fondly fingered the collar. Then her husky deep voice broke the spell Serena had fallen under.

"You like it?" she asked. "Josh gave it to me," the woman added while she openly let her eyes roam over the curves of Serena's body. Serena could feel the blush converging over her features and was helpless to do anything about it. Before she thought to speak, Jenna continued. "Please forgive my rudeness upon your arrival. I was waiting for Josh's approval."

Approval? Approval for what? Serena silently wondered. Josh waved them into their seats. Once they were both seated, he once again took his.

"I can tell by the look on your face that you have questions. I'd also venture to say that your questions aren't only professional in nature," Josh said to her before continuing. "Please allow me to explain. Jenna is my wife, my love. She also happens to be my submissive. She was a bad girl yesterday, part of her punishment is that she cannot speak today unless given permission to do so."

Part of Serena bristled at what the man across from her just said, but the look of love and contentment written all over Jenna's face quickly changed her mind.

She longed to ask Josh what the rest of Jenna's punishment was, but didn't dare.

As if reading her mind, Jenna reached out and began to stroke the back of Serena's hand. It was an odd sensation. Never before had she been touched by a woman. It wasn't repulsive, but it didn't arouse her either.

When Josh did the same to her other hand, she fought the need to pull away. His slight touch raised chill bumps that ran the length of her arms. He was a man in control, one who would ask and expect to be answered.

How she knew, she had no idea. It was a feeling she had, just the same as the feeling that the man across from her could be trusted. His every movement, every touch, proved the love and respect he felt for his wife. His feelings were obvious and ran deep.

"Have you ever been spanked?" Jenna asked quietly leaning closer as she did.

For a minute, Serena was struck dumb. Did she have a darned sign stamped on her forehead or something? Did it say *I want to be dominated* or *spank me*?

"N-no," she croaked.

"That's what the rest of my punishment was. That was what you were wondering wasn't it?"

"Yes," she admitted through suddenly parched lips.

"First he made me remove my clothes and then I was told to kneel before him. With my elbows on the floor and my bottom in the air, he used my favorite paddle. The sting burned forever," she said in a hushed voice. "But then he took me in his arms and made love to me, long and slow."

Oh god, she could feel her blush deepen and spread. Great! How professional would she seem now? Serena was having a heck of a time controlling the urge to grind herself into her seat. Just the low-lidded look on their faces was enough to make the room feel ten degrees hotter. Not to mention what it did to her dry panties.

Stifling a groan, she opened her mouth to speak, but was abruptly cut off by the firming of Josh's grasp upon her hand.

"I don't know who he is or if he even exists for you yet, but I can see it in your eyes. In the way you carry yourself. You crave to be dominated, it's written across every feature of your face. The way your face is flushed, the color riding high on your cheeks. It's in every breath you take."

His voice was soothing, almost coaxing in its deep sensuality.

The circles his finger was making on the back of her hand punctuated every word he spoke. "If you have no one and are ready to delve into your submissive side, Jenna and I will be glad to help you."

Holy moly! She couldn't get a word out, but it didn't matter because Josh wasn't done. "You would like that, wouldn't you, Serena? I could see it on your face as you watched Jenna's fingers stroke the gift of my possession. A gift I bestowed upon her the first night she completely submitted to me. Would you like to wear proof of my possession too, sweet Serena?"

"Uh," she couldn't get her brain to form thoughts much less coherent words. "I'm in a relationship right now, but thank you anyway."

Not sure of what to say, Serena decided to stay where she was comfortable. "What type of website were you looking to have designed?"

Josh gave her a knowing smile. "We own an online adult business. Part of the site is free. In this part, we offer free stories, personal want ads and general information. The paid area of our site is an adult store where we sell pretty much everything you can think of." He gave Jenna's hand a gentle squeeze, she continued where he left off.

"I've been the webmistress since we opened, but I can no longer keep up with the traffic and my other duties, so we decided to hire someone to rebuild it. We surfed around and kept coming across your name. Would you be interested in working for us?"

The whole way home Serena could not stop thinking about Josh and Jenna. They were so different and at the same time they were…normal. In a way, she wished she would have asked some personal questions. They seemed open to discussion. Several times her curiosity had almost gotten the best of her.

* * * * *

Several days later, Zane lay in bed, his laptop computer set across his thighs. Sounds of the modem connecting awoke Serena. She stretched her hands above her head rolling toward the muffled sounds.

"Zane?"

"Hmmm?"

"When you finish what you're doing, would you give the new site I'm building a once-over?" she asked through a yawn.

"Sure, Rena," he said, head bent forward, fingers flying across the keyboard.

Serena mumbled out the web address, rolled over and before he could ask questions, she was once again sound asleep. Surely, he'd heard her wrong? No longer able to concentrate on the work in front of him, Zane saved the file and typed in the address Rena had just given him.

Without even a glance at what the site had to offer, he scrolled to the bottom of the page. Sure enough, right there for all so see was her name and business e-mail address.

Zane chuckled, he wondered how his straitlaced, prim and proper Rena had been roped into building an erotic website?

He couldn't hold back his curiosity so nudging her shoulder, he woke her up. "Rena?"

"Yeah?" she answered sleepily.

"How in the world did you end up with this job?" He couldn't help the amusement lacing his voice. Evidently, Serena also heard it because she sat up in bed and gave him a harsh look.

"Don't get all bent out of shape, babe. I'm just saying it's hardly you."

"Would you just look it over, Zane? I didn't ask for your opinion, just your help. Click on the links and browse around and make sure everything is working." He held back his chuckle knowing damned well she was pissed.

When he started checking things out, she added. "Besides, when I met with the owners the other day, they didn't seem to mind if I was the type. Since they propositioned me, I'd say they didn't mind at all."

After dropping that bomb, she promptly rolled over showing him her back.

"What in the hell do you mean they propositioned you?"

He watched as she once again sat up in bed. The bedspread dipped low around her waist completely baring the top half of her body to his view.

The filmy pink tank top she wore wasn't nearly thick enough to conceal her nipples. The darker brown of her areolas circled the pink tips. His mouth watered thinking about what he wanted to do to them. How he wanted to suck them deep into his mouth, tugging and tonguing until she was mad with need.

Forcing his gaze from her breasts, he decided that now she just looked plain annoyed.

"Just what I said. Just because you think of me as a geek doesn't mean someone else might not find me sexy." She was on a roll now and there would be no stopping her. "The owner and his wife asked me if I'd like to spend some time with them. I told them no, of course."

"Of course," he mumbled more than a little unnerved about someone else wanting what was his. When Serena scooted lower on the bed to lie down, he stopped her.

"Let's look it over together?" he asked.

She nodded her head in answer.

The next thirty minutes or so was spent checking the site over. The graphics were just amazing. Explicitly erotic. Some were home shots of the average housewife while others looked more professionally done.

Beside him, Rena gave a groan of what could only be embarrassment at a detailed photo of a couple engaged in oral sex.

Just looking at the photos had him hard as steel. The few times he'd glanced at Serena made him even harder. Her face was flushed a rosy red, her eyes seemed to dart around the room while snatching quick glances at the screen of his laptop. She couldn't seem to sit still. Her squirming movements beside him only made matters worse. His arousal was at an all-time high. And dammit, he knew if he didn't let her off the hook now he'd embarrass them both. Besides, she was a good sport sitting by his side the whole time even though it was obvious she was uncomfortable doing so. The least he could do would be to let her go back to sleep.

Settling a chaste kiss on her brow he said, "Why don't you go ahead and go to sleep? I'll finish looking it over and let you know tomorrow if I found anything."

When she'd settled in, he took up where they had left off.

Well, she'd asked him to take a look around, so that was exactly what he would do.

The site was an educational experience. For a man who loved to dominate his women sexually, he was a bit surprised by the amount of traffic the site generated. Were there really that many people out there interested in pushing the envelope? It was sort of like a balm to know he and his brothers weren't the only ones out there who preferred more than straight vanilla sex.

He clicked on links to make sure they worked, reading all the while. When he came across a section devoted entirely to personal want ads, he decided to take a peek. There were many options, much more than any newspaper could boast. Depending on your lifestyle, sex and sexual orientation, to name a few, you could find anything or anyone you ever dreamed about.

Zane clicked on a link that took him to ads for single submissive females. There were hundreds of them. All short, sweet and to the point. That was one thing about the Internet—inhibitions ran low. People felt comfortable to let loose, to say things about themselves they might not be able or willing to admit face to face.

As he scrolled the page, some of the ads leapt out at him. The things some of the women wanted seemed barbaric. He couldn't picture himself physically hurting a woman. A lot of pleasure and a tiny bit of pain could bring a woman to an explosive orgasm. The right combination could make a woman beg and plead for more.

Closing the page for submissive singles, Zane decided to take a peek at what type of ads dominant males were submitting. Once again, he was struck by some of the out-there posts he was reading.

Before he could comprehend completely what he was doing, he typed out an ad of his own. What would it hurt? No one would probably answer, he told himself. And if they did, well, he would deal with that when the time came.

His conscience warned him. The steady, deep breaths of the woman lying next to him reminded him, but he couldn't give up such a chance. When opportunity knocks, you answer the door.

Unsure fingers quickly finished the ad to his specifications. The cursor flashed over the send button, there was no fighting it.

The need within him was overwhelming. His cock strained against his sweatpants, nudging the underside of his laptop. For so long he'd fought the truth. Tried to hide from the fact he was different. He should have known he couldn't hold back the beast forever.

Hell, just talking to his brothers on the phone was enough to bring on a raging erection. The three of them had always been close, but once they became sexually active, that closeness blossomed. He missed his brothers. Moving home seemed more promising every day.

Back in the now, Zane clicked the button. It was done, the message was sent. Now for the wait. There was no guarantee it would even be answered.

He could always answer some of the others. Now that he had taken the step, brought the possibility within reach, he knew there was no going back. He was beyond the point of no return.

Soon he would have to give consideration to Rena. How could he tell her the reason for their split? How could he not, she deserved at least that much. Guilt ate at him.

He couldn't do it. The one ad was enough. If he didn't get an answer back, he would have to think of something else, but for some odd reason he wasn't worried about it. Something about the ad he placed felt right. Without analyzing it, Zane decided to just go with the flow.

Chapter Two

&

Serena stared out the kitchen window watching, wondering. The past week swam through her mind as her still shaky knees led her to a stool at the breakfast bar. Lord have mercy! The fingers of her right hand traveled over a love bite marring her tender skin. It was unlike anything Zane had ever done to her.

Excitement and apprehension flowed through her veins in remembrance. Her body longed to be completely taken in the same way as he'd started to earlier in the day.

The feelings were new and frightening. Never in a million years could she picture stuffy, straitlaced Zane as the aggressor. They always sort of just came together. Until just a few minutes ago, their relationship had been based on convenience. Nothing more, nothing less.

He'd come out of nowhere, silent as a slight breeze. She didn't even know he was there until she felt the length of him pressed to her back.

Within moments, the unmistakable presence of his jutting arousal was nudged snugly against her backside. In reaction, her body began to tremble. It took no more than his touch and her imagination to cause such an immediate response.

Serena lost count of how many scoops of coffee she was at as Zane's large hands ran the length of her spine. The light pressure at her back caused her to lean slightly forward.

Serena could hear Zane's ragged breathing. It sounded much like her own.

Take me dammit. Take me! Her mind screamed and yet she couldn't force the words from her lips.

Splayed fingers snaked around her front. Finding her breasts, they squeezed and plucked at already pebbled nipples. A small whimper escaped her throat a second later when she felt a sharp nip on the tender skin where neck met shoulder.

The pain was brief, but intense, leaving her breathless. Her heart raced with the possibilities. Combined with the heat of his cock rubbing against her bottom and the fingers rolling her nipples, her knees could no longer hold her weight. They finally buckled.

Had it not been for the close proximity of Zane, Serena was sure she would have melted to a puddle right there on the kitchen floor.

A string of muttered curses cleared her head and brought strength back into her legs. When she felt able, she turned to look at Zane.

"Son of a bitch," he said. "I'm sorry, Rena. I...I... Aw, hell!"

Serena watched as emotions played across Zane's face. Self-loathing flashed quickly as well as, what? What was that? Guilt? He felt guilty for what had just happened. Serena wanted to laugh, or cry. She wasn't sure which. He felt guilty and all she wanted was more. Why in the hell couldn't she just tell him how excited she felt. How hot she was. If he'd only check for himself, the wetness of her panties, the slick juices coating her pussy were surely proof enough.

Working up the nerve, Serena opened her mouth then quickly closed it. She tried again then shook her head to clear it. She'd just managed to pry her still shocked lips apart when Zane pushed his hand through the waves of his brown hair, spun on his heel and stalked out the front door.

Still sitting at the breakfast bar, she let her mind wander over the past week. At first, she thought it had all been her warped imagination. Tiny changes no one else would notice, but she had.

Things as simple as slight mood changes. Zane seemed to sit with a brooding look on his face. Something he'd never done before. His normal happy-go-lucky self had become deadly serious on more than one occasion. Another facet of Zane Serena had never before witnessed.

Smoldering eyes spent a lot more time following her as if studying her the way a scientist would study a specimen. It was disconcerting. He seemed to be battling some sort of internal conflict.

The whole thing only brought closer to the surface just how far apart their relationship was that Zane didn't feel he could talk to her. And at the same time, she didn't feel as if she could go to him and ask what was wrong. She often wondered if this was the beginning of the end for them.

Those were some of the things she would love to change. Another was the fact that during the past week Zane had become violently aroused on several occasions. She'd even noticed it last night when they had gone over the website together. That was something she was enjoying and didn't want to see change.

And yet, he hadn't even so much as kissed her.

Today was the first day he'd acted on his severe state of arousal. That he'd shown any loss of control. It made Serena wonder just what she could do to nudge him in the right direction.

Even if she could push him, what would it accomplish? It would probably just make things worse. If she backed him into a corner, forced him into taking her the way she wanted to be taken, he would probably run.

Later that same afternoon, Serena sat in front of her computer remembering a past that haunted her. A past that was always just a thought, a nightmare away.

How could she want so desperately to once again attain what had taken all her will to break away from?

It won't be the same with someone who loves you, she reminded herself.

Getting married so young was not the problem. The problem was that her ex-husband had been a sick bastard. His sole purpose in life was to humiliate her.

At first, Serena thought his commanding presence to be exciting. The thought of being tied to his bed, of being loved recklessly, had heightened her arousal. That was before her dreams had become reality. A reality she wouldn't wish on her worst enemy.

It was before the man in question taught her never to trust. To never give herself completely to man or woman, emotionally or physically. It had been a lesson learned the hard way. One she'd fought tooth and nail.

She wondered if she would ever again be the carefree soul of her youth. The answer came quickly. There was no going back, only forward.

With her head bent, Serena began doing the final checks on the erotic site she was finishing up. After an hour or so of surfing from page to page, she couldn't help but take one last look at the *Single Doms Looking for Single Subs* page. Many posts were new. The site had an enormous amount of traffic, but one post in particular caught her eye. It was a Dominant man looking for an intelligent, independent woman with submissive tendencies.

He went on further to say she must be willing to give over all control in the bedroom.

Serena scanned the rest of the ad, her heart beating double time. She scanned down until she could read his username then scrolled to the bottom of the board until she could see who was online. He was active.

Her breath caught as she made her way to the chat room he was logged into.

* * * * *

A week later as Zane made his way to his office, he was still mentally kicking his own ass. Things just seemed to get worse by the day.

Damn, damn, damn! What in the hell could he be thinking? His body ached with need. Good god, he could still feel the soft curve of her ass cheeks as they'd warmed his straining erection. And it had been damned near a week since that little episode.

A week of torturous hell.

A week of doing everything in his power to stay away for fear of devouring Serena whole.

A fierce need to take her right where she stood had set his feet in her direction before his brain had thought to engage.

Switching on his computer, he made his way to the coffeemaker.

During the past week, Zane had fought himself. Fought his needs. He was like a hunter stalking its prey. And because of their living arrangement, Serena had become his prey.

He no longer felt happy when he looked at her watched the movements of her luscious body. No, now he felt unrelenting heat. Barely contained lust he was having a hell of a time hiding. The online conversations with the submissive woman who had read his ad only made matters worse because now he realized just how bad off his relationship with Serena really was.

Cup of coffee in hand, Zane settled in front of his computer and as was becoming habit, he logged into the chat room where he would meet ESKAY. It was a private chat room. The moment her username popped onto his screen, his cock hardened and lengthened.

How's it going? he questioned.

Real good, and you? she answered. Polite conversation wasn't at all what he was in the mood for. Right now, he wanted to hear her deepest, nastiest secrets.

All is well here, but it'll be even better as soon as you start sharing more of your fantasies with me. The cut of his slacks left him much needed room, which was a good thing because just the expectancy of more of her stories was enough to make him come.

You with me? he typed when she didn't answer.

Yeah, I'm here. What was it you wanted to know?

He could tell from how slow she was responding that she must be nervous.

I want to hear all of them, eventually, but for right now, your naughtiest will do.

Several seconds ticked by before there was an answer.

Well, I want to be made to submit. You know that, but I also want so much more.

There was another pause before more words began showing on his screen. *I've not tried very much so I guess you could say I'd like to try it all. One of my biggest fantasies is to be spanked.*

Oh hell, his palms itched at the thought. His raging erection was turning into a monster insisting on release. Lowering the zipper of his slacks, he palmed himself. The feel of his heated skin within his own hand made him think of insisting ESKAY experience the same.

What are you wearing right now? Typing with one hand was slow going.

Wearing?

Yeah, darling. What are you wearing? Whatever it is I want you to take it off and play with that pretty pussy of yours just as I'm stroking my cock. I want you to tell me piece by piece what you've removed.

No new message flashed across his screen. Was she removing her clothes or was she thinking? Hell, for all he knew she'd left. Damn, this was frustrating!

I just unbuttoned my blouse, popped up on his screen. His cock did the same, popped up, that is, at the typed words.

Now what, your bra?

I'm not wearing one today, only a white lace chemise. Oh, shit! He wondered if her nipples were puckered and pressing against the lace. Were they petal pink or a natural brown, maybe just a shade darker than the rest of her skin?

It's off too, as is my skirt. Now I'm only wearing my panties and hose.

What kind of hose?

The kind that stop at the thigh, but they're not held up with garters. They're white with lace tops.

His hand worked the length of his shaft in an up and down pumping motion as he read her words. He tried to picture her, what she looked like based on the description she'd given him, but couldn't seem to do it.

For some reason a woman with sparkling green eyes and lustrous strawberry blonde hair kept popping into his mind only it wasn't the woman he was chatting with. The woman who kept invading his thoughts was Rena and it made him feel guilty as hell.

Pushing away the guilt, he continued to work his length with one hand while typing directions to her with the other.

Leave the stockings on, but remove the panties...slowly. Pull them down while thinking about the width of my cock. Try and picture how it'll be the first time I spank your ass until it's red and hot. How you'll squirm and cry out every time the palm of my hand lands on your flesh. If she were there with him now, he wouldn't be able to hold back. He was having a hell of a time controlling it now, and he was alone.

Think about how good it'll be the first time I tie you up and take you. Can you imagine it? I can. I hear your cries of pleasure in my sleep as I dream about forcing every inch of my cock into your tight hole. Both of them. Eventually I'll take you every way there is for a man to have a woman.

Panting with excitement. The need to release overwhelming as his spine tingled. His balls were drawn up close to his body as if seeking comfort and release.

When the word *done* flashed on his screen, he almost lost his load.

Now tell me how you want to be spanked.

Oh, god, she typed. *I want to be stripped or made to strip. I've seen it in my mind so many times. I've dreamed about it.*

And after you're stripped? he prodded getting quickly closer to his own release.

After that, I want to be placed over your knee. To feel your strength beneath me. Then I want you to make my bottom burn. I've read it will make me burn not only on the outside but on the inside also. Do you know if it's true?

Holy hell, he wasn't going to be able to hold out for much longer. His grasp grew steadily stronger around the flesh of his staff as his hand jerked up and down.

You making yourself wet, baby? I want you to come while you talk to me. I'm almost there myself.

I am...oh, I am. She typed. Normally everything she did was in perfect English. Complete sentences. It was strange to see a fragmented post, she must be close. How he wanted to be there with her.

Now, baby. Come now. Pumping his hand, he did so himself. Shuddering through his release, he vowed that the next time they wouldn't be talking online. Next time he would be seeing her face. Up close and personal.

The time was getting close. Soon they would have to meet.

Later that day, his thoughts reverted back to Serena and all that had happened between them over the past week.

How he would catch himself watching her. The force of his arousal was instant as he pictured all the things he wanted to do to her. Different ways to make her beg for more.

He was sure she would be disgusted if she could take a trip into his mind. A faint flicker of interest had quickly crossed her face, but interest in what? She could have no idea of the things he would do to her. How he wanted to push her to the limit and then push her some more.

He could imagine what her face would look like when he told her step-by-step what he wanted to do to her. Her parted pink lips would glisten as her tongue peeked out to moisten them. Cheeks flushed with desire and shock only made the paleness of her complexion that much more intense. The woman looked shocked, confused. If given half the chance, Zane would keep her that way.

There was no use in trying to keep the animal at bay. Soon he would sit Serena down and tell her what was in his heart. In his mind.

Guilt had become a big part of his day. There was so much to think about, it made his head throb. Should he tell Serena of his cyber-relationship now or after meeting *ESKAY*?

If he told her now and gave her the choice, would she choose to submit? If she chose not to, wouldn't that make things easier? He would no longer have Serena to worry about. He would then be free to follow through with finding a woman to fill his life. One who would relent in every way thinkable. So why did the thought of not having Serena in his life bother him so much?

Fingers pinched the bridge of his nose trying to keep the monster headache away. There was no time to delve into his feelings just now. He had a choice to make. Would he tell Serena about the mystery woman before or after meeting her?

God, he needed to talk to his brother.

There was just something about Hayden's slow drawl that could soothe the wildest of beasts. Picking up the phone, Zane punched in the numbers that would link him with his big brother. With home.

"Yeah," a voice answered on the other end of the line. Zane's brow creased in confusion. The voice was Hayden's but it was anything but calm.

"Dammit! Is anybody there?" the voice growled. Yep, it was definitely Hayden's voice.

"I'm here. What in the hell's wrong with you?"

"Hey, baby brother. How's it goin' out there in sunny Californ-I-A?" It was a standing joke between the O'Malley brothers how Zane had opted to move far away in order to get out from under their father's thumb.

"Sunny," he answered feeling better than he had just a few brief moments ago.

Zane could hear something in the background. It sounded suspiciously like a screaming woman. And possibly even glass breaking.

"What in the hell is that, Hayden?"

"Oh hell, don't mind her none. It's just The Hellion and she's done got herself in trouble with Judge Gumar again."

"Austin?" Zane couldn't help but chuckle. They had aptly named her The Hellion when she was about ten years old. All of a sudden, Zane felt even more homesick.

"What she do this time?"

"Her and that damned car, tearin' up the roads, sellin' her wares," he added in a disgusted voice. "Judge told her she could either have a real job by the end of the week or she could spend thirty days in jail. She opted for the job and I needed a bookkeeper."

This time there was no chuckle about it. Zane's laugh was outright loud and obnoxious. The thought of Hayden, the rough and ready rancher and Austin, The Hellion, thrown together on a daily basis was almost more than he could imagine.

When the background noise got too loud to hear the phone conversation, Hayden hung up saying something about an ass whoopin'.

Ten minutes later, when Zane settled in front of his computer, he was still wiping tears of laughter from his eyes.

The click of the mouse sent him to the private chat room where he'd been meeting his mystery lady, *ESKAY*. Slowly, methodically he read over each message she'd left him, each fantasy she'd shared. It probably wasn't wise to save them, but he couldn't seem to help himself.

ESKAY knew he was in a long-term relationship, she admitted to being in one herself. Further conversation between the two revealed neither was completely happy. They were looking for more. They talked about their lack of communication with their partners and how it had caused a gap that could not be comfortably bridged.

ESKAY insisted she was looking for a monogamous relationship, not a fling. How happy he'd been to hear that. At the age of thirty-two, Zane was ready to settle down. After being married for a few years, he looked forward to starting a family. Life would be grand. All he needed was a woman who shared his ideas and views on life. A woman he could communicate with in every way.

Once again, his mind wandered to Serena.

He could picture her long strawberry blonde hair flowing over creamy bare shoulders in a mass of curls. Her green eyes could bore a hole through to the heart of any man. Eyes that had witnessed too much at a young age.

His revelation would hurt her. Zane couldn't remember a time where he'd given a shit about a woman's feelings enough to worry whether breaking off a relationship would cause her pain.

He didn't want to start now, but it seemed he had no choice in the matter.

He would meet the woman first. However things turned out, he would be completely honest with Serena. A deep breath whooshed out of full lungs as he turned his gaze back to the computer screen in front of him.

The click of the keyboard sounded in the noiseless room of Zane's office as he typed out a message.

It's time we met. I cannot wait a minute longer to see if you are who I've been waiting for. Tomorrow at noon on the corner of Ocean and Cape at a small pub called Patrick's. We'll talk then.

ZAOGUARD

His hand fisted after sending the message on its journey through cyberspace. There was no going back now. No returning to the life he'd led for the past four years.

It would be a new beginning. Zane replayed in his mind the phone conversation with his brothers. The excitement in their voices when they found out he soon planned to move back home. His heart rate increased at the thought of once again being close to the two people who meant the most to him. And since he was being honest with himself, the thought of seeing his father again wasn't nearly as bad as it used to be.

After the death of their mother, the O'Malley brothers had been inseparable. Returning home as a wealthy man would be nice. No longer would he feel the need to prove his worth to a father who had once felt let down by the fact that none of his sons chose to follow in his footsteps.

A small envelope flashed on the bottom corner of his computer screen notifying him of incoming mail. His pulse sped. This could be it. With another click, the message was open. Zane began to read.

I know where it is. I'll be there.

ESKAY

Damp palms slid along his slacks. Soon. Soon he would meet the mystery woman who could make him feel whole again. His conscience was nagging him, but not nearly as much as his cock. He hadn't seen the woman yet. Had never heard her voice and yet his body was responding. He was hard and ready. In need.

In need of control. To feel a warm body pressed tightly to his. Hands bound and out of the way. Totally at his mercy. It was such a heady thought to know that the possibility of a dream come true was so close at hand.

Zane's chair squeaked as he levered himself up, stretching the kinks out of his six foot sinewy frame. The snip of the lock clicking into place filled the room. Fully engorged, Zane lowered himself back down into the chair parked in front of his desk then lowered his zipper. It may have only been hours since he and ESKAY had gotten off while chatting, but he couldn't seem to help himself. He was so hard he hurt.

The teeth of his zipper grated along his throbbing sex as it was slowly lowered. His fully erect cock sprang free of his trousers. Its engorged head glistened with a drop of pre-cum as his large palm fisted its length.

Damn, but he needed the woman now. He needed the feel of a hot mouth gliding over his unyielding length.

A slow sigh fell from his lips as his head fell back against the chair. The rhythm of his hand caused his hips to buck. Up and down, squeezing and tugging, he brought himself closer. He kept his eyes closed, allowing his mind to wander.

Long hair shielded the face of the woman kneeling in front of him. His hands tangled in her hair as his hips rocked to and fro, his cock delving deep into her mouth.

"That's it, baby. Just relax and take me."

The heat of her mouth, as he imagined it would, inflamed him. His grip tightened as the woman submitted. Hands bound behind her back made it impossible to keep her balance with the quick thrusts of his pelvis.

His hold on her head would keep her right where he wanted her. In his mind, he could see the bliss on his own face. He could see his lips moving, he would be giving directions. Commanding her to do as he wanted.

"Suck me. I'm going deeper, Little One. Relax your throat and take all of me."

The woman's face was still hidden from his view. What would she look like?

Would her eyes be closed lightly, dark lashes sweeping the contour of her cheeks? Would she look him directly in the eye if he demanded it of her? The thought of staring directly into the windows of her soul as he exploded in her mouth kept him teetering on the edge. It would be a dream come true.

Serena had always avoided eye contact, keeping her eyes tightly closed during sex. Even though she never balked at oral sex, she also never offered to swallow or watch.

If the woman he was meeting worked out, she would consent to both. There would be no hiding, no holding back.

"Open your eyes, baby. I want to watch." If she didn't immediately respond, he would give the hair wrapped around his hand a tug until her eyes found his.

The sensations grew as his hand continued to stroke and tighten. Keeping himself on edge, but holding off the inevitable. Sweat beaded on his upper lip. Close, he was so close.

"Oh yeah…oh honey, I'm going to come." He would then pull back until just the head of his shaft remained in her mouth.

"Here it comes, baby. Take all of it, swallow it all," he groaned as his balls drew up with the imminent explosion. Then he came in the warm recess of her mouth holding her head in place as she worked frantically to swallow all his body offered.

His free hand fumbled for tissue as the other hand worked furiously between his legs. Once, twice, on the third stroke he broke. A low groan, ripped from the back of his throat, echoed off the walls as he tightened his hold, milking the last drop from his semi-rigid length.

At the same time, the face of the woman in his mind was revealed. A devilish smile curved a full, sassy mouth. Emerald green eyes sparkled as she licked her lips.

Just as quick, she was gone, but not before he recognized her.

Serena.

Oh, if only his Serena could be the same as the Serena he so often dreamed of.

Chapter Three
ഔ

Serena faced her reflection in the mirror. It was not a pretty sight. After a long, sleepless night, she was left with dark shadows under her eyes. Her complexion was drawn, haggard-looking.

A hot shower would surely work wonders. If not, she was screwed. She pushed all thoughts of her lunch appointment away. Right now, she would focus on making herself presentable. Put all of her concentration into a relaxing morning.

After clearing the breakfast bar, Serena padded silently up the hall. Back in the bedroom, she stripped off her nightgown and panties. The full-length mirror hid nothing. Turning her back to the mirror, she looked over her shoulder.

The pale skin of her back seemed almost transparent. Never one to sunbathe due to fear of burning, her skin stayed a milky white. It seemed that no amount of sunscreen was enough to keep her fair skin from turning lobster red.

Freckles lightly covered her shoulders. With a critical eye, Serena let her gaze roam lower. Average was the first word that came to mind. Never had she considered her shape or assets to be above average. That was okay, she could deal with it.

Many times in her life, she had heard that if she only dressed more fashionably, or more provocatively, she would gain more attention.

As a businesswoman, she only wanted to seem professional. As a woman, she wanted to be noticed. There was a time when low-cut blouses and tight skirts were the norm for her. Then she had met Zane. As she got older, more comfortable, she no longer worried much about how she dressed, except when it came to business. That would all change today, she thought as she eyed the green slip dress hanging from the closet door.

Its thin straps would show off her shoulders. The rounded neckline would show just a hint of cleavage. The store clerk had assured her the length of the dress would enhance her legs.

To finish off the look, she had picked out a lacy white thong and lace top thigh-highs. Spiked heels would round out the look and make her calves look great. Now if only she could gain the confidence to wear an outfit so unlike what she normally wore. Thoughts of the silky dress caressing her bare bottom made her shiver. Her skin grew hot. She could feel the moistness begin between her legs. She squeezed her thighs together in an effort to ease the growing pulse there, but it did little to help.

Leaning over, Serena turned the faucet until the water temperature was just right. As the large, circular tub filled, she settled herself. Warm water caressed every smooth curve of her body. She felt light and carefree, except for the yearning deep inside.

A yearning she could no longer ignore. The round tub was one of the reasons she so loved the house she shared with Zane. Four years ago, she had thought it would be a relaxing place to get away. Then as time wore on, Serena often hoped Zane would join her, only he never did. Recently though, as her hunger grew, she was often thankful for the positional jets placed around the sides and bottom of the tub.

Serena pressed a button on the side panel, which caused the jets to come to life. Bubbles tickled her hardened nipples as she positioned the streams of water right where she wanted them. Her hips rocked in unison to the needy pulse within her. With her eyes closed, she could pretend the fingers plucking her nipples belonged to Zane. The hand snaking slowly up her thigh to nestle against her pink folds would take what it wanted without explanation. Serena could feel the cream of her body even as she was surrounded by warm, bubbling water.

Panting through shallow breaths, her body shuddered through its release. It was better than nothing, but far from enough.

With the edge taken off her sexual frustration, she rose from the tub and quickly dried herself. Donning her robe, she strode into the bedroom to sit in front of her vanity mirror. One look at the clock told her just how much time had passed. Now she would not have nearly enough time to prepare.

It was probably a good thing Zane had left for work so early. She would have had a hell of a time explaining why she'd spent an hour in the tub.

Pulling the brush through her already drying hair until it was tangle free, she turned on the hairdryer and went to work. The constant hum of the machine could not mask the beating of her heart. Being nervous was not something Serena enjoyed. It made her feel vulnerable, an emotion she wasn't used to dealing with.

Serena could not believe what she saw in the mirror. After drying her hair, she artfully arranged it high on her head. It was supposed to be a sophisticated look—instead she looked as though she'd started out as a runway model only to end up as a green-eyed siren.

Her hair looked mussed, as if a man's fingers had fought the pins controlling her curls. Wisps of hair had already escaped the entrapments and were curling gently around her jaw. One in particularly unruly curl was lying nestled in the shadowed valley of her breasts.

That single curl stood out in sharp contrast to the deep green of the slip dress just covering her body. Its length landed just above the knee, but hugged every contour. A slit up the right side continued to mid-thigh giving off a wicked glimpse of leg. The shoes were much higher than the conservative pumps she normally wore, but they were sexy.

The feel of soft fabric against bare skin made her core heat. Her nipples pressed into the fabric making the unruly lust coursing through her body even more intense.

Even the slightest movement caused friction. It was heaven and hell all rolled up in one.

The drive across town was full of misgivings and excitement. This meeting was extremely important to Serena. It could mean a change in her future, a big change. Would it be a change for the better?

There was so much to be unsure of and yet, at the same time, if she didn't at least try she would never know. No, this was not something she could back down from.

It seemed weird to feel so unsettled after being comfortable for the past four years. It wasn't until recently that Serena realized being content wasn't nearly enough. Some days she wanted to scream from the sheer monotony of the situation. She had been pushed in no way, not to love or to hate. She was merely there and it was no longer enough.

Soon she would be forced to look deeply into her heart. To see where things would stand with Zane. Were the feelings deeper than they appeared on the surface? If so, why had she never given more or expected more?

She knew the answer—the difference was that never before had she been willing to admit it. She vividly remembered the day she told Zane of her past. How she had been married as a teenager to a man she loved with all her heart only to learn he felt no tenderness or love to return.

She'd always dreamed of marrying a strong man. Her gift to her husband would be her virginity. Never in her wildest dreams could she have imagined a more ruthless bastard.

It wasn't long before Serena learned that her husband couldn't care less if she was a virgin or not. In the bedroom, he treated her no better than an animal and out of the bedroom he ignored her. The naïve dreams of a new bride didn't last long in their house. Neither did her sunny disposition. It didn't take long to turn her into the cynic she was today.

Some of the things he had expected her to consent to still made her shudder. As a young, untried woman, they had frightened her to death. She wasn't sure how she'd managed to hold on as long as she did.

Hopes of love were doused and depression had taken their place. If only he'd loved her, she would have done anything for him. It took her a while before she realized that a man who loved his wife would not live to humiliate her. Once she'd learned that valuable lesson, Serena had left never to look back.

The past and her knowledge of what could happen is what made everything so confusing. It was hard to understand why when she was finally in a relationship where things were calm she would want to give it all up to a dominant who would push her to the limit. The desire was so fierce she could not back down from it. Soon she would make her decision.

* * * * *

Zane scowled at the computer screen, staring at the flashing cursor that sat still. He couldn't concentrate to save his life and he was weary. Sleep had eluded him again last night. Was he doing the right thing?

Guilt ate at his gut. Serena's face flashed before him. The woman he lived with was a comfort, but did he love her? He wasn't sure. Even if he did, would it be enough? Could love take place of the physical and mental needs he would be missing as a dominant?

It was almost time to meet her. The muscles in his shoulders were tense. The broad expanse covered by a button-up shirt. The top two buttons left undone exposing a small amount of tan flesh.

Feeling a bit uneasy, Zane strode to the restroom adjoining his office. The sight to greet him in the mirror was a bit intimidating, he admitted to himself. Damn! If he didn't get a grip and relax he would scare his submissive off before they had the chance to get to know one another.

His normally smooth chin was covered with dark stubble. Disheveled brown hair reached just to the top of his collar. One disorderly curl hung rakishly over his forehead. Intense hazel eyes, currently the color of weak tea, were positioned below thick brows. Not normally a vain man, Zane gave himself a last once over before he slipped into his tan sports coat.

Zane decided to walk the two blocks, allowing himself some time to think. The weather was neither hot nor cold. He could easily do without all the traffic and the noise that went along with it.

That was one of the things that made it so tempting to move back home. Not only would he be close to his brothers, but he would be out of the city.

Early on, city life had been fulfilling, but not any longer. Now it felt stifling. Too much traffic. Too much noise. It no longer held any promise. The idea of moving home brought along with it a whole new set of circumstances. One thing at a time, he muttered to himself. *Let me get through today then I'll focus on the move.*

Once he reached his destination, he pushed through the heavy wooden door. The interior was dark, and it was like a second home. His early days in the city had been lonely ones until Patrick O'Connor had taken him in as a friend. Now everyday he spent his lunch hour with Pat. The white-haired pub owner was a stout man of undetermined years. His heavy accent told of his Irish upbringing. Zane was sure a friendlier, more loyal friend could not be found.

The inside of the pub reminded him of O'Malley's, his brother Sean's place back home in Texas. It was probably one of the reasons he felt so comfortable there.

"Hey, O'Malley," Pat called. "Will you be having your usual today?"

"Not today," Zane answered. At Pat's questioning glance he added, "I'm meeting someone."

Pat gave a wink and a knowing smile as he skirted his way back behind the bar. "Fine then, lad. You just be lettin' me know when you're ready."

Zane picked a booth in the far corner of the room. It was shadowed and fairly private. His fists clenched and unclenched in an attempt to release some of the tension coiled in his body. It didn't seem to be helping one bit. He couldn't understand why on earth he was so nervous.

It wasn't like he was going to take the woman somewhere and start right in.

They would talk and get to know one another before things could progress. Then if they were compatible and in agreement to the terms they'd both set forth during their brief cyber relationship, they would proceed.

Zane would not allow things to go any further than talking until he opened up to Serena. His throat worked furiously past the lump there at the thought of causing sweet, unassuming Serena pain. He would also ask the same of *ESKAY*.

She would have to break free of the relationship she was currently involved in if she wanted to go any further with him. It was something they'd already agreed upon, but he would be sure to bring it up again because once he found a submissive to love he would never let her go.

He watched absently as the lunch crowd milled around while he casually sipped at the glass of water Pat had insisted on delivering to his table.

Every ounce of his willpower was currently being used to keep his baser needs at bay. He wanted to pounce on the woman the minute she walked through the door. At the moment he could care less what she looked like, or even what she wanted or needed. He had an almost overwhelming need to dominate. Just the thought caused his cock to thicken. Thoughts of a woman bound increased the pressure behind the zipper of his slacks. At least one good thing came out of his change of dress since becoming a businessman and living in the city. There was a lot more room behind the zipper of slacks than there was behind the button fly of a pair of jeans.

He'd given some consideration to dressing like he used to. Jeans instead of slacks, and a Stetson to cover his unruly waves. Replacing his loafers with a pair of comfortable boots would be great, but that look was of the past. Not something he'd given into since leaving Texas four years earlier. Soon enough though, he would be back home. And as the saying goes...when in Rome.

He chuckled a bit. He could only imagine the look on Serena's face. She would probably have to be reminded to pick her jaw up off the floor when she finally saw him in his cowboy clothes.

The last thought was like a bucket of ice water. Thinking of Serena while meeting with another woman was more than enough to cool Zane's ardor, leaving him with emotions he wasn't quite ready to deal with.

Zane checked his watch. Five minutes after the hour, which meant she was five minutes late. If she were already his submissive, he would surely have to think of some way to punish her for her tardiness. His idea of punishment was completely different from what he'd read of other dominants.

The idea of hurting or humiliating never entered the scene in his mind. Instead, he would tease and tantalize until she begged for release, then make her wait. A good spanking could also prove useful if both parties were to consent. There was much to talk about between them before a relationship could begin.

Many ideas had been gathered from the Internet. A large number of Dom/sub couples signed contracts specifying what they were willing to do. A safe word would need to be agreed upon. He had even prepared a sexual questionnaire for *ESKAY* to fill out. It would help him better prepare for their time together if he knew her likes, dislikes, things she was willing to try and others that were completely off-limits, before they took the next step.

Just as his mind moved back to sensual punishment the front door opened. The silhouetted figure standing just inside the door was very familiar. His pulse increased as the figure moved further into the room. His eyes raked the lone form from top to bottom then slowly back up again. No way! It couldn't be, but it was.

"What the hell!" Zane swore as he rose to his feet. Raking a large hand through his hair, he moved away from the booth and into the light. The sight before him took his breath away.

Spiked heels covered tiny feet. Sexy as hell legs were encased in thigh-high hose. He knew they were thigh-high because he could see a single lacy top peeking out the side slit of her dress.

A dress that left bare as much as it covered. Green soft-looking fabric hugged every curve of the voluptuous braless body. Beaded nipples begged for release from the confines of the low-cut bodice that was held up as if by magic by extremely thin straps.

What caught his attention most of all was the wide-eyed angelic face staring back at him. He knew every curve of her body. Instant recognition of the slight smile tilting her soft bow-shaped lips brought every nerve in his body to full attention. Upswept hair looked as though it had been thrown carelessly together. It was perfect. About the time she finally spoke, it finally hit him. This was his woman!

"It's you," she whispered. "Oh, my god, Zane! It's you."

Chapter Four
∽

Sit or fall, those were pretty much her options. Her head felt light, and emotions ran rampant through her overloaded brain. Serena moved, her legs shaking so badly she wasn't sure she would make it to where Zane was standing.

"I need to sit," she said. It was all that was necessary evidently because Zane was by her side instantly, helping her into the seat of the booth. He slid in next to her and watched as her eyes lowered abruptly blocking his view of the emotion-filled orbs.

She couldn't bring herself to look up. There was so much to think about, her mind couldn't grasp it all. She drew a blank. For that brief moment, she probably couldn't have remembered her name to save her life. It was a strange feeling. More than likely a defense mechanism.

Slowly, it was all coming back. She wanted to be angry, but at what? Yeah, he may have placed the ad, but she was the one who answered it.

Had he been meeting with other women? Did he answer other ads? The idea hurt more than she could imagine. It felt as if a fist had gone and squeezed off her air supply at its source. When had she become so emotionally attached to Zane?

She peered at her white knuckles as she brought her hand up to her mouth. Serena then pushed the tiny fist against her teeth welcoming the small bite of pain. It shook her enough to keep the keening wail from escaping. What in the world had she done? And why now? Why must she only now realize she was in love?

Holy shit! Love?

"Oh, no," was muffled behind the hand still at her mouth.

"Stop that!" Zane said sternly. "You'll hurt yourself, Rena."

She felt the warmth of his hand as it tugged hers down and patiently unclenched her fisted fingers. Once done, his large hand did not release her, instead the thick, hair-smattered fingers intertwined with hers, holding her tight.

How could a basic touch feel so intimate? The heat radiating from his body made her skin sizzle. Her hand felt hot where his palm was pressed tightly to hers.

So much of the past few weeks suddenly made sense. The fierceness he had showed her in the kitchen. The sexual aggressiveness that was not usually present. The feeling of drifting apart from him, it all made perfect sense now.

Finally, Serena felt strong enough, brave enough to look up into Zane's face. Starting at the thick cords of his muscled neck, she worked her way up. His square jaw looked stubborn. It was something she'd never really noticed. He seemed much more tenser than the easygoing man she was used to. The right side of his lip curved just the slightest bit. It wasn't really a smile, but it helped to ease her nervousness. Bronzed skin was stretched taut over strong cheekbones and a straight nose, but it was his eyes that held her. Hooded, hazel eyes stared back with a hunger like nothing she'd ever witnessed.

Goose bumps appeared on her arms and a shiver ran the length of her spine. Serena's body wanted to take over. Its fight or flight system was evidently malfunctioning because she didn't know whether to run far and fast or throw herself in his arms begging him to take her home.

She sensed his inner turmoil when his hand tightened almost painfully on hers taking the choice from her. The corner of his mouth curved the tiniest bit higher. Between the wicked little grin and the twinkle in his eyes, Serena was lost.

His voice broke the silence. "Rena, I never knew…"

He couldn't seem to go on. Instead, he continued to watch her. His intense perusal of her face left her shaken.

The skin covering her thighs tingled with anticipation. Memories of their shared e-mail confidences flashed before her. Things she had only ever dreamt about. Things she had never felt comfortable telling another living soul. She could remember what he wrote as if it were in front of her.

If this works for us you will belong to me, I will settle for no less. I will use your body and bring you great pleasure in the process. My will, will be your will.

How could the man sitting next to her have written those words? They were nothing like what her Zane would have written. He was laid-back, a man not afraid to compromise. The e-mails she'd received were from a commanding presence. One used to being obeyed. Could two such personalities live inside one man and did she want to find out?

He already seemed so different. If she gave herself to him the way her body craved, the way he would now insist upon, could they ever reclaim their carefree selves? For some reason she didn't think so.

Over the past few weeks, so much about him had already changed. It brought home just how much she didn't know about the man whom she'd lived with the past four years.

Zane was watching her. His hazel eyes raked over her as he waited. The flash of heat within those eyes bore right into her soul. She would never again be free, she would never escape. Serena feared that from this moment on she would do whatever he asked of her. What if he asked too much?

"Don't look at me like that, Rena," Zane growled. "If you keep it up, begging me to fuck you with those wide, green eyes of yours, I'll do just that no matter who is watching."

Her gasp was audible. "Zane!" she cried while looking around to see if anyone might have heard.

His smile was slow coming and then its strength was torturous. Her mouth had attracted his attention. In her nervousness, she licked her lips then jumped at the growled curse Zane released.

"Damn Rena! I won't warn you again," he said in a deadly calm voice.

She could feel her eyes widen as her hands began to shake. Lord, what in the world had she gotten herself into? Quickly, she looked away. She wasn't sure what she was doing wrong, but evidently it was making Zane angry. In the four years they had lived together, not once could she remember a time when he had been truly angry.

"I don't... I mean... I'm not sure wha—" She was cut off by Zane's deep baritone voice.

"Don't, Rena," he said soothingly. "It's not just you, baby, it's both of us. We have a lot to talk about. I want to get that over with now, okay?"

It might have been phrased as a question, but Serena felt it more as a demand. They *would* talk now, she bristled a bit at that thought, but he was right. Now was just as good a time as any. With a nod, Serena gave her answer.

"I still can't believe it's you, but now that I know, we need to get things straightened out. You do realize we can never go back to the same old dull routine?"

Still unable to speak, Serena once again nodded.

"As I'm sure you now realize, I'm not the man you thought I was. It's been a hell of a long four years hiding my true self from you. I wanted to protect you, especially after you told me about your ex-husband, but now that I know what you want and need, there will be no going back. If you want out, say so now, Rena, because once I have you where I want you, I'll never let you go."

Serena couldn't quite swallow past the lump in her throat much less talk. Realizing she loved the man sitting next to her had been a surprise. The timing was way off and it left her at a disadvantage. Vulnerable. "I don't know, Zane," she whispered hating the weakness in her voice. "I don't know you anymore."

"You know all the important stuff, Rena." She watched as a brief flash of panic crossed his features.

"It's my sexual preferences that are new to you, nothing else. I know what you like, baby. What your wants and needs are. You know I would never hurt you or force you, but I won't lie to you, Rena. I'll push you every step of the way."

He wasn't leaving anything out. Laying it all on the line. Right up front so there would be no confusion. There could be no turning back. "I can be rough. Damn, but it's been hard holding myself back. I'll challenge you every chance I get. Just as we talked about in our anonymous e-mail, you are your own person in all aspects of your life, but in private, you will belong to me. I won't go back, I can't. Not now, now that I've read your fantasies. Now that I know what you crave."

"Oh, god," she groaned aloud. Her fantasies! How could she have forgotten the things they had shared during their time online. Things that were much easier said while typing at a keyboard. She could feel the slow burn in her body. The heat in her cheeks was nothing compared to what she felt between her legs.

* * * * *

Zane watched as a flush worked its way up Serena's neck and into her cheeks. He could only imagine what the rest of her body would look like all pink and pretty.

It angered him to know that they'd wasted so much time dancing around each other. The fact it had taken for the both of them to go as far as looking for another to fill those needs upped his blood pressure.

He watched as she once again licked her lips. His mouth ached to taste her, but now was not the time. Now was the time for answers.

"Tell me what you're thinking, baby."

"I know what we—what we shared in our e-mail," Serena cleared her throat. Zane could tell by her flushed cheeks that her embarrassment was mounting. "I meant it. All of it, but that doesn't mean I'm not afraid, Zane."

"Afraid of what?" he asked as he rubbed the back of her hand with his thumb. The normally warm skin felt chilled, her eyes seemed a bit panicky.

"Mostly of myself, I guess. Of my feelings, my needs. I'm not sure if I can put myself in this situation again."

Zane's eyes narrowed. He didn't like where this conversation was going. "It took me a long time to trust again, to find myself. Now I'm used to doing pretty much what I want, when I want. I don't know if I can give that up."

"First of all, don't ever, and I mean *ever* put me in the same category as your lowlife ex. We may not have had the best relationship these past four years, but I believe I deserve at least that much. Now, as for the rest—I'm not asking you to give up your life, but I will from this day forward demand total obedience in our private life. Can you live with that?"

He could tell she wasn't sure, at least not one hundred percent sure. Her emotions were plain for all to see. Of course, he hadn't given her much choice.

"I can try, Zane. That's all I can promise."

"It's a start, Rena and for now that's enough." He felt triumphant, it was just the tip of the iceberg, but it was a start.

Fear and frustration were evident in the way she held her body so still and stiff. As if she might shatter at the slightest move. He wouldn't ease her fears just yet. Fear of the unknown could be a good thing. It would increase the intensity of her arousal while honing her senses.

Senses he wanted to send into overdrive. Of course, that would have to wait because Pat chose that moment to collect their order.

"Have you decided what you'll be having, O'Malley?" he asked.

"Hey Pat, you remember Serena, don't you?" Zane said in way of a reintroduction since Rena had only been there a few times before. Serena, polite as always, murmured the appropriate response. Once the introductions were made, they ordered their meal. Zane ordered a beer for himself and a piña colada for Serena. For several minutes, they sat in silence.

Zane watched Serena. She was tense, the air fairly oozed with it. When she started to fidget, he decided to break the silence.

"Tell me Rena, why did you never say anything to me?" He was trying not to sound angry, but wasn't at all sure he was accomplishing the feat. The amount of time they had wasted left him feeling deep displeasure.

"I'm not sure. I mean, for the first few years I was content, happy with our relationship. After my ex…" When he scowled, she backtracked. "I mean…well, it took me a while to trust again. Once I was able to trust, I felt as if something was missing."

He wasn't sure who or what his anger was aimed at. He wanted to rage, to yell and pound his fist into a solid object at the thought of how much time they had lost. How they'd almost lost each other over their lack of communication. What a loss that would have been.

"Why didn't you say anything once you trusted me? Why look elsewhere?"

Her coral-tinted lips opened, but no sound escaped. He watched as she lowered her eyes as if to close out the outside world. That was something he would no longer allow. If things were to work, they would have no more secrets.

A knuckle placed just under the center of her jaw lifted her chin. Once her eyes settled on his, she opened her mouth.

"I could ask you the same. About looking elsewhere, that is."

She was completely right.

"I can only tell you how I feel, Rena. I don't know if it will answer your questions or not. When we first met, I spent every daydreaming about having you. I wanted you at my mercy, bound to my bed." He watched as another soft flush stole over her delicate skin, but refused to stop. She would know it all.

"I have always had different sexual preferences which is one of the reasons why I'd never been involved in a long-term relationship before we met. I need to possess. I want to brand you as mine, Rena and now that I know you want the same, we can never go back.

"It had originally been my plan to seduce you slowly. To show you all that I could give you, especially after I had a taste of you. I knew right away we would suit each other. Then, our first night living together, you told me about your ex-husband. I knew then I couldn't follow through. I didn't want to pressure you, but I also wasn't prepared to lose you so I tried to change who I am. As you can see, it didn't work."

He watched as his words slowly sunk in. The awestruck look on her face. "You did that for me?"

The words seemed to stumble from her mouth. Her clear green eyes glistened with tears. "I was embarrassed, and afraid. I knew that if things continued the way they were it would only get worse. I felt ashamed to tell you what I wanted, what my body needs." With a wobbly smile and a nervous giggle she continued.

"You have always seemed so cool, aloof almost. Our relationship was more congenial, never passionate. I was afraid you would think less of me if you knew." He opened his mouth to speak, but Serena held up her hand to stave off his words.

"Now I know that isn't so, but I didn't at the time. I was willing to look elsewhere for my physical needs because no matter what our relationship was like, I didn't feel complete. Please understand though, I never would have been unfaithful to you. I would have come to you before going further than a meeting."

Zane believed her, she'd said as much in her e-mail. He was still completely baffled by how he could have missed such intimate details about her. Had there been clues? It was almost too much to take in.

His fingers itched to feel the warmth of her skin. Once again, his large hand engulfed her much smaller one. He could feel the slight tremor that shot through her, making his cock twitch. Seeing her so compliant, so willing to share her thoughts made him horny as hell. There was definitely no turning back now.

Chapter Five

෨

Two hours after their revealing lunch, Serena realized there was no way in a million years she would be able to concentrate on work.

Every nerve ending sizzled at the thought of what was to come. Her stomach was coiled tight and damned if the mere though of Zane tying her up didn't drench the clean pair of panties she'd just put on.

A giggle escaped her lips. She was a nervous wreck. The anticipation was almost unbearable. Tonight would mark a new beginning for both of them. It continued to amaze her.

How could she be frightened and still have no doubt as to the path she would choose? The thought of being dominated brought so many emotions to the surface. Emotions she had tried to suppress.

Tonight would be special, a new beginning for the both of them. Serena saved what she was working on, then shut down her computer.

The rasp of soft carpet beneath her bare feet let her know that she had made it to the bedroom. One look at the huge bed and her mind began to wander. How would he want her? Would he prefer her on her back, her legs spread wide so he had easy access to her center? Her breasts would also be ripe for his touch.

Or would he want her on her stomach, her hips elevated on pillows, allowing him access to the tight virgin entrance of the one spot he'd never tried to take her?

Zane. His name whispered through her mind. Even though he was at work, she felt closer to him than ever before. She felt her body sizzle with heat from deep within just begging to be released. It was going to be one hell of a long afternoon. What was a woman to do with so much time on her hands?

Serena made her way to the foot of the bed where she sat on the edge. Her hand slowly made its way over the gentle swell of her stomach then continued on its journey between her aching breasts.

With her head thrown back, hair trailing behind her, Serena rolled her nipple between her thumb and finger until it beaded to a diamond-hard point.

While the one hand relentlessly fondled her breast, the other zoned in on the warmth at the apex of her thighs. Firm pressure on her clit caused the muscles in her upper legs to jump. She could smell her own arousal. Feel her dampness through the slacks she wore.

If only I had the time, she thought to herself. *Then I could do a proper job of releasing some of this tension.* But time was something she was running low on. If she planned to make tonight a night they would never forget, she would have to start now.

Paying attention to the opposite breast, Serena brought herself closer and closer. Thoughts of Zane and the possibilities tonight could bring gave Serena the last little push needed to drive her over the edge.

A gentle wave of sensation moved through her until her back arched and her hips bucked against the hand between her thighs.

When her breathing returned to normal, Serena changed her clothes, grabbed her bag and left the house. So much to do and so little time to do it in.

There was so much she wanted to experience with Zane. Some things that still made her feel ashamed or frightened and yet she couldn't seem to get them out of her mind.

It was hard to come to terms with something she'd always seen as the dark side of herself, but Serena vowed she would follow through with it. No way was she going to back out now.

She wondered what she should pick up for tonight. During the short time she'd spent with Zane at lunch, she had gotten a glimpse of the type of man he really was. Should she take the initiative and buy some of the adult toys she had dreamed of using during their lovemaking? If Zane were really a dominant man, would he insist on doing the shopping? Oh hell, she couldn't make up her mind.

To stay on the safe side, Serena decided to stick with a nice dinner and some sexy lingerie. Her mind went through a mental list of what was needed for Zane's favorite pasta dish. When all the ingredients were in the basket, she headed to the checkout counter throwing in some candles along the way.

Groceries were soon unloaded into the backseat. A loaf of fresh French bread rested along side a tiny bag containing satin and lace from a small boutique located just up the street.

Her heart was pounding, palms sweating. The anticipation was going to give her a coronary, she thought as her pussy clenched, leaking more of her natural juices, soaking another pair of panties.

She hoped Zane would like what she'd planned. The thought of aroused hazel eyes watching from under lids heavy with desire sent what felt like tiny fingers walking up her spine.

I can do this. I can do this, she told herself over and over, as she parked the car and unloaded the groceries. When she finished, Serena took a glance at her watch then she headed to the bedroom to prepare.

First a warm bath was drawn. Vanilla scent was added to the water making the air in the bathroom not only relaxing but also very sensual.

Wisps of cream-colored satin and lace were removed from the bag. Once the tags were removed, the tiny garments were carefully laid on the bed. Then Serena removed her clothes and sank into the soothing warm water.

Eyes closed, trying her hardest to relax her body, Serena wondered if Zane was having as hard a time. Maybe he was sitting at his desk aroused and ready. Was he as hard as she was hot? Every little touch to her own body sent fingers of desire up her spine. Maybe Zane was doing the same, masturbating to release the pent-up tension of what tonight held.

There were so many questions that needed answered. Things she forgot to ask during their lunch. Several of the messages Zane had sent talked about his brothers. About plans to move back home in order to be closer to his family. He often talked about Hayden and Sean, but she had never met them. Was he serious about moving? If so, would she be welcome?

So many questions and no answers. Serena pushed away the nagging fear of being left behind instead focusing all her effort in preparing herself for Zane.

The fluffy towel felt like heaven as she rubbed her still wet body. Once she was dry enough, Serena sat on the edge of the tub with a bottle of lotion in hand.

The lotion smelled good enough to eat and felt like silk as she smoothed it over the satiny skin of her legs. With a quick comb of her wet tresses, Serena wrapped her towel around her, securing it in the center of her chest then stepped into the bedroom.

Waiting was hard, but not knowing what to expect was even worse. Would she be able to handle what Zane expected of her? The challenge of his stubborn chin had been unmistakable. Disturbingly intense. He would insist upon total submission. Could she do it? Could she follow him to such an erotic destination? One, that could either end with astonishingly wonderful results, or a seriously shattered heart. With her body leading the way, there was only one answer. Yes!

* * * * *

Damn! Damn and double damn! If he didn't get out of the office he was going to go fucking nuts. He had tried. More than once as a matter of fact, but there was just no way in hell he was going to be able to work knowing damned well Serena was at home waiting for him.

Nerves made his shoulders tense. Anger still flowed through his veins. He completely understood where they were both coming from so no blame was being placed. It just seemed so stupid that they'd been dancing around each other all this time. What a waste. It was time he could have spent with Rena getting her used to his ways. Training her to please him and pleasuring her in the process.

The thought of his Rena wearing the wide gold chain he planned to have designed for her melted the anger he held within. He knew the perfect jeweler for the job. By the time it was ready, she would also be ready.

Zane had seen it in her face. Flashing green eyes could no longer hide the hunger she'd buried so deep. Nope, no more would there be secrets between them.

Zane left his office early, wicked thoughts swirling through his mind. It was time. He had to know just how far Serena was willing to go. In order to do that Zane would need a plan. One was already taking shape it just needed a little fine-tuning to be successful.

Using the backdoor to the local adult bookstore brought Zane into a large room. Shelves held every type of sex toy imaginable. Remembering the e-mail where Serena had told of her fantasies would help him pick the right products. Soon he had a basket filled with the things he considered necessary.

He gave a mental wince as the cashier totaled his purchase. Whew! Prices sure had gone up in the past four years. Of course, it was money well spent if he could make even one of Serena's fantasies a reality.

All the way home, Zane thought of the contents in the plain brown paper bag on the passenger seat. Vivid images thundered through his head like a stampeding herd of cattle. Images of how Serena's body would accommodate not only the jewel blue vibrator, but also the lifelike dildo.

In preparation, he'd purchased a small anal toy and a tube of lubricant. The sooner her body was ready, the sooner he could take her there.

Vivid images of her body filled to capacity with not only his length but also one of the toys made the wait seem insurmountable. But wait he would, until Serena's body was ready. Until she could physically, mentally and emotionally handle the loss of control that would inevitably come with the type of possession he had in mind.

He could hardly wait to teach her how to pleasure herself with his benefit in mind. Would it take her long to learn to control her release? To hold on until he commanded her to come. There were many lessons to be taught and learned before she could truly be his submissive.

He would proceed slowly and cautiously and yet, at the same time, his determination was at an all-time high. His eager cock, which was causing a substantial tent at the front of his slacks, seemed to pulse in time with the beat of his heart. A beat, that just happened to be following a double time rhythm at the moment.

The aching arousal of his shaft combined with wicked thoughts was enough to make Zane's mouth water. Because he knew that where some lessons would be taught, some would also be failed. It was the prospective failures that made the palm of his hand tingle.

Would Serena really go through with it? In one very specific conversation, Serena had talked extensively about being spanked.

The thought of pulling her warm, wiggling body over his lap after exposing her full, rounded ass cheeks made him groan. Watching her skin turn pink, knowing she would be wet and hot with her arousal almost sent his car skidding off the road.

Damn! Get a grip, Zane. If you don't kill yourself trying to get home, you'll surely end up scaring her to death.

With much effort, Zane slowed his car to a more normal, less illegal speed. Then he cleared his head of wicked thoughts instead replacing them with calculated lesson plans and memories of home.

Upon reaching the house, Zane noticed that not only was Serena's car in the drive, but all the blinds had been drawn closed. So, his sassy-mouth, soon-to-be submissive wanted privacy, did she? He briefly wondered if she would be surprised that he'd decided to come home from work early?

Zane grabbed the bag off the front passenger seat and made his way to the front door. Using his key, he let himself into the house.

Wonderful smells assaulted his senses before he even got close to the kitchen. Garlic and fresh bread were among them.

As always, their home was clean, nothing out of place. Zane set the brown paper bag on the end table and made his way up the hall.

His sense of smell was still being challenged, only this time it was something much more sinful than garlic and fresh bread.

It was the smell of woman. His woman. The smell was comfortable, soothing. Just the same, as it had been for the past four years. He hoped this was one aspect of their relationship that could remain pretty much the same. It was like coming home to a warm summer day even in the dead of winter.

Would she be dressing, he wondered as he continued on his journey up the hall. What had she chosen to wear? Would it be the comfortable white cotton briefs that hugged her every curve or a sexy thong that made him want to jump her without the benefit of foreplay? Knowing the contents of her drawers, it could be anything in between.

Finally, he'd made it. He was standing in the hall in front of their closed bedroom door. Should he knock and wait as he normally did when he knew damned well she was dressing or should he jump right in to their new Dominant/submissive roles? He decided on a compromise since they had yet to talk through all the details of their new relationship.

He knocked and then without waiting for an answer opened the door and let himself into the room where he was drawn to a standstill just inside the door.

A stocking clad foot was perched on the edge of the bed while small hands rolled cream-colored silk up an equally pale thigh. He was sure at that moment his face must have looked like that of a schoolboy with his first glimpse of a skin magazine. After schooling his features, Zane said in a cool, controlled voice, "How far do you intend to push before I push back, baby?"

He knew damned well she'd heard him enter the room and yet made no move to cover herself or to change the purely sexual pose she still held. Not that he wanted her to.

It was just the fact that she was already playing him. Pushing to test their new boundaries. To see how far she could go before something happened.

Zane had an idea that the next few weeks would prove to be damned interesting.

With every ounce of willpower left, Zane skirted the opposite edge of the bed until he was facing Serena. Once there, he settled himself into a chair trying with all his might to keep an unreadable look on his face when really he wanted to whistle and howl like the horny man he really was.

Serena's gaze snapped up to where he could see it, the blush of her cheeks told a tale all their own.

"Zane," she said. "You're home early."

Not giving an inch, as a sort of test, Zane nodded his head and said, "Continue."

He watched as she cocked her head to the side and narrowed her eyes just the slightest bit. She did that when annoyed, it made his lips curve at the corners.

"Continue?" she finally asked.

"Continue," he repeated not giving an inch. "Where you left off, Rena. I'd like to watch."

The blush once only covering her cheeks now made its way down her throat until it beautifully covered the uppermost swell of her breasts.

When her slightly shaky hands started seductively rolling a stocking up the other leg, Zane knew he was lost. He may be able to teach Serena to be his submissive and with proper training, he might even be able to dominate her body and own its every release, but in the grand scheme of things, she was the one who held all the power. It was a sobering thought.

Following the movement of her hands, Zane for the first time, noticed the rest of her outfit. It was new which told him she'd made the effort to go shopping today.

For some strange reason it made him happy that she would take the time and make the effort. Especially given the fact that she probably didn't figure she'd be wearing it for long.

Well, he would just have to make sure she had the chance to keep it on. Maybe her first lesson, and his as well, would be patience.

The camisole top had wide straps, which seemed to lightly caress her shoulders. The low-cut lace curved with her breasts playing a game of peek-a-boo with dusky nipples that were begging for attention if their tautness was any indication.

The silk of the bodice shimmered in the subdued light of the room making it look like falling water. The shorts bottoms were cut high showing the most tantalizing view of curves he'd ever witnessed.

All-in-all, the outfit covered more than most bra and panty combinations, but good god did she look sexy as hell!

Moving to the closet, Zane pulled out a thin wraparound dress he had only seen her in on a few occasions. It was sage green in color. Its design caused the side slit to open to about mid-thigh while sitting and showed off her lovely cleavage.

The only thing holding the dress together was the thin belt that would wrap snugly around her waist.

Moving around the bed, Zane handed the dress to Serena. He watched as she eyed the skirt and blouse she'd evidently already picked. When she looked back up at him, he merely raised an eyebrow in challenge.

Once again, she narrowed her eyes causing a small furrow between her brows.

Oh yeah, this was going to be fun. His gut clenched with arousal. His cock anticipating every moment of Serena's training because, from now on things would be Zane's way.

Chapter Six
෨

Fingers trembling, Serena took the dress from Zane. Inside she bristled. It was a test—she knew it. She was well aware that he knew she would get ticked because he'd picked her clothes out when it was something she'd already done.

Not quite sure how to deal with the whole situation, Serena looked up into Zane's face. His expression was inscrutable, all except for the slightly raised brow and a twinkle in his eyes showing his amusement.

She could feel her anger rise and opened her mouth prepared to give a sassy retort. The change in his eyes was instantaneous. One second there was merriment and the next cold steel. A tremor of awareness flashed over her skin as Zane moved closer.

Without a thought, Serena took a step in retreat but it did no good. As if he were stalking her, Zane moved slowly, silently closer. He matched her step for step until she was backed up against the hard frame of the bathroom door.

The bite of pain and the overwhelming sensations of pleasure exploded through her body as Zane's large hand tangled in her hair, tugging until her head was angled right where he wanted it.

Her mouth opened on a gasp as he moved closer. Lips almost touching, Serena could smell the mint candy Zane favored.

Just as she though he would kiss her, he said. "Don't push, baby. We have a lot to talk about, a lot to work out."

She wanted to argue, about what she wasn't exactly sure. The man was driving her insane. Couldn't he just throw her on the bed and have his way with her already? Hell, if he'd do that she'd be willing to talk about anything.

Serena opened her mouth to say as much but never got the chance before warm lips were pressed to hers. Slow and deep the kiss went, until she could no longer remember what she'd wanted to say.

Once again, her head was angled so she was staring right into the face of her lover. "Do you understand?" he asked.

Lowering her lids, Serena could only nod her acceptance. Slowly, she felt Zane's hand fall away. For a second, she just stood there. Staring. Waiting. Then he said "Get dressed, Rena. I'll be waiting. You did make me dinner, didn't you? Those wonderful smells have to be coming from somewhere."

Oh, crap! Dinner! She'd been so caught up in the moment, she'd already forgotten. With lightning speed, Serena finished dressing.

Once in the kitchen, she finished the final preparations for dinner. Her body tingled and ached with its need for release. Bat-sized butterflies had taken up residence in her stomach and she wasn't exactly sure she would make it through dinner without begging Zane to take her.

She squeezed her thighs tightly together trying in vain to dull the throbbing that had taken over her swollen clit, but it didn't help. She felt so hot and so sensitive.

With each passing minute, Serena's anger mounted. Damn it! Did the man have any idea what he was doing to her?

With everything ready and hands full of food to be carried to the table, she turned and ran right into Zane.

The breadth of his chest was like slamming into a wall and almost knocked her to the floor. Sinewy arms stretched out to catch her, trapping her against his hard body.

Great! She couldn't keep her mind off of him as it was and now she'd have to start all over. Trying to cool down with him in the same room was almost as impossible as keeping her panties dry.

His face showed much more calm than any man had the right to be and it pissed her off. She could feel the flush of anger on her cheeks and was having a hell of a time keeping her tongue in check.

Evidently, Zane was aware of her inner struggle. His mouth curved ever so slightly at the right corner and his eyes, although still watchful and intense, showed the slightest twinkle.

"Relax, Rena." His voice low and gravelly.

"Relax? Yeah — sure. Whatever," she answered a bit peeved at herself for not being able to hold onto her composure the way he so easily seemed to be doing.

"Don't get sassy, Rena. We haven't had a chance to talk yet, but I bet I could find something to keep your delectable mouth occupied until you have the chance to calm down."

His voice was seductive and commanding all at the same time. He may be trying to soften his censure of her attitude, but she had no doubt he meant every word.

Taking a deep breath, she said. "Ok, Zane." Then handing him a bowl, she added, "Here you take this and I'll get the salad."

Placing the bowl of salad on the table, Serena asked, "Wine?"

After pondering the question for a moment, Zane nodded. She'd just made it back to the table and was pouring wine for the two of them when Zane signaled for her to stop. She looked up, not sure what was wrong when he said, "Just one, Serena. I want you sober for tonight."

She wasn't at all sure if this is what she'd signed up for. The use of her full name let her know he would accept nothing short of total capitulation. Her body was on edge, her mind confused. What else could she do, but wait and see what the night had in store for her?

With dinner in full swing, Serena watched as Zane ate with gusto while she was barely able to swallow a bite here and there. Mostly she just pushed the food around her plate. Waiting. For what, she wasn't sure.

From the corner of her eye, she watched Zane. His movements were conservative, fluid. Like a sleek animal ready for anything. The muscles of his arm bunched as he brought each forkful of food to his mouth reminding her of his strength.

Her stomach fluttered and her heart rate increased when he finally wiped his mouth and pushed his plate back.

Tentatively, Serena lifted her head. Zane was watching her. His hazel eyes seemed to be looking straight through her, it made her uncomfortable. It took all of her willpower to resist the need to squirm and wiggle in her seat.

The silence grew as his gaze bore into her. Just when she thought she could no longer handle it, he spoke.

"We have a lot of things to talk about, Rena, but first I just want you to listen."

She could feel the smirk on her lips. She'd never really been one to sit quietly by and listen and was ready to let loose with words to convey that thought when Zane added, "Not a word. Do you hear me? I've got some things to say and you'll sit and listen until I'm done or I'll tie you to the chair."

Realizing that tying her down would do little to keep her mouth shut, he added, "Lips closed or I'll find something to occupy them with."

He took what looked to be a deep, calming breath then added, "I warned you not to push me. I won't repeat myself. After I've said what I need to, then we'll talk."

Serena watched as Zane pushed himself away from the table and stood. He paced a few steps then turned to face her from across the room.

The slight stir of air created by his movement caused his scent to drift over her.

Musk and man clung to her nostrils causing her mouth to water. His biceps bunched beneath the sleeves of his shirt as he clasped his hands behind his back. The movement caused his shirt to pull tight across his chest. A chest her fingers ached to stroke.

She couldn't pull her gaze from his body. To look into his eyes just now would be a big mistake because there was no way she could hide what she was feeling. The longing. The need, it was integrated into every cell of her being.

* * * * *

The slight tremble of her hands where they lay in her lap made him want to hold her tight, but it couldn't happen just yet. There was so much to get through before they could start their new lives.

With his hands clasped tightly behind his back, where they would remain so he didn't drag her to him, he stood across the room from her. Her eyes burned him everywhere her gaze touched.

How would she react to what he was about to say? Would his demands be too much for her to handle? His stomach clenched and his heart ached. The thought of losing Serena nearly drove him to abandon the new life he had planned for the two of them.

He was leery of pushing too hard too fast due to her background, but knowing what he knew about her secret fantasies, her deepest desires made him move ahead. Really, he had no choice in the matter. They couldn't go back and keeping things the way they were wouldn't work so forward was the only option.

When she continued to keep her eyes averted, he went to her and gently tilted her chin. After he was sure he had her complete attention, he once again moved back clasping his hands behind him.

"We talked about many things in our online conversations. Because of those chat sessions we know more about each other now then ever before. I won't ask you to stay until I'm sure you know exactly what you're getting into."

He tried to choose his words carefully. She needed to know everything he expected of her.

"I'm not the man you thought I was, just as you aren't the woman I thought you were. There is so much more than we could ever have imagined. Now that I know this, things can never go back to the way they were.

"If you decide to stay with me, Rena you need to know this. I'm a hard man. I want all of you and I won't settle for less. I know what you like, what you're willing to try and what your fears are. I'll never intentionally hurt you, but I will push you and just when you think you can go no further, I'll push you a little more."

Some of her fantasies echoed in his ears. He would make them all come true, if she would let him.

"I'll have total control of what happens behind closed doors and even some of our outside relationship, but I don't want a robot, Rena. I want a woman who isn't afraid to tell me what she needs and wants. A woman with opinions and thoughts.

"I may not agree and I'm sure we'll have our share of arguments, but we'll work it out." He tried to keep his voice level. If she knew just how hot he was and what he intended to teach her, she would probably run far and fast.

"Don't get me wrong, baby. If you push me, I'll retaliate. You may not always like your punishment, but if you trust me, you'll understand."

It took every ounce of his remaining willpower to keep the ice out of his voice. "I'm not and never will be like that sorry bastard you married. I know deep down you're aware of the difference or you wouldn't be here, but I had to say it anyway."

Her eyes had grown wide. He was sure a little of it was fear of the unknown, but from the way her breath heaved in and out of her bowed lips, and her nipples tightened to little points against the thin fabric of her dress, he was sure just as much of it was from arousal.

"There is one other thing we talked about in our e-mail, but have never spoken of. I've been giving some consideration to moving back home. I want to be closer to my family, my brothers and my father. If you decide to stay in this relationship, you'll be going with me. Once I have you Rena, I won't let you go. So be sure, give it some thought and let me know once you've made your decision."

He prepared for the worst and hoped for the best. Her green eyes glittered with moisture and she opened her mouth to speak, but nothing came out. Kneeling down to eye level, he took her hands in his and held tight. "It's okay, baby. Tell me. I'll listen to whatever you have to say. As I said earlier, I may not like it, but I'll always listen."

This time when her soft, pink lips opened everything seemed to spill out at once.

"I've been doing nothing but giving our online conversations thought, Zane. There is nothing here for me without you. I want to be yours, but I have to know that I can also be myself. I trust you with my body, but I don't know that I'll ever be able to give one hundred percent of myself to anyone ever again."

He watched with narrowed eyes as a small, wobbly smile curved her mouth. "So, when do we move?"

With purposeful strides, Zane walked around the table. When he was finally behind her, he turned her, chair and all, completely around until she was facing him. Placing both hands on the table on either side of her chair, he lowered his head until his mouth was scant inches from hers.

"We move as soon as we have our affairs in order."

He tugged at her full lower lip with his teeth causing her to gasp then lapped away the sting with the tip of his tongue.

"And make no mistake, Rena. You'll be mine. One hundred and ten percent all mine. I won't settle for anything less." With those words barely spoken, he took her mouth in a kiss so hungry he thought he might explode.

Serena arched her back tearing her mouth from his in the process. He felt her small, panting breaths where her face was buried at his neck.

"Zane," she said on a winded whisper.

"It's all right, baby. Come to me. Let me take you where you've only dreamed of going." His hands gripped hers, bringing her to her feet. He gave her little choice but to follow.

When they reached to doorway to their bedroom, he took notice of her flushed cheeks. Her eyelids were heavy, the green of her eyes glazed with lust. Just the way he wanted her, he thought with much satisfaction.

"Serena, look at me."

It was a command growled low into the silence of the room. When she looked up, he held her in place with a hand at each side of her face. His thumbs brushed lightly over the smooth skin at the corner of her eyes.

"If I do something you don't like, I want you to tell me. Do you understand?" When she hesitated to answer, still staring into his eyes, he leaned forward and once again nipped her bottom lip. This time no tongue followed to soothe. Her eyes widened and became a bit wild, wary.

"Answer me, Rena. Do you understand me?"

Her head started a forward motion as if to nod, but he held her still. "Tell me what I want to hear, Serena. I'll ask only once more. Do you understand me?"

"Yes," she answered in an exasperated voice that made him struggle to hide his smile. "Yes, I understand you."

"If you want me to stop what I'm doing at any time, for any reason, simply say *stop*. We'll then discuss what the problem is. If it's something that doesn't bring you pleasure, I'll never ask it of you again. You'll have to be the one to bring it up. If you're just unsure, we'll talk it out and it'll be your choice whether to continue or not."

He watched her face as what he said sank in. "If you just need a breather, I want you to tell me. We'll talk about it, but I can't guarantee I'll always allow it. I may want to make you come until you beg for mercy. It'll be so explosive you won't know what you were begging for."

It was as if her feathers ruffled. Her eyes flashed a wicked green and he could see what effort it took for her to hold back what he was sure would be a sharp retort. There was something about the word *allow* that didn't sit right with her.

It amazed him just how much he enjoyed seeing her in a snit. He could almost feel the sting on his palm, as it surely would the first time he placed her facedown over his knees and paddled her sassy little ass. Zane held tight as she tried to back away, wiggling free of his hold. Oh yeah, this was going to be very, very interesting.

Chapter Seven

ഇ

Serena's heart thundered in her chest. Her head whirled with all that had taken place. Her knees felt jelly like yet strong enough to carry her weight as she turned and fled, heading back toward the kitchen. She knew Zane would follow. The sound of his curt steps on the tiled floor rang out like shots through the silent room causing Serena's heart to bead wildly.

Serena stopped when she reached the kitchen counter. Facing away from Zane, she tried desperately to calm herself. Her trembling hands griped the kitchen counter where she stood staring out the window. The white of her knuckles gave away her unease even while she struggled to slow her ragged breaths.

The man had changed so completely it was mind-boggling. He seemed larger than life. Like he'd morphed from your normal, average Joe into a true-life, macho dominant in a matter of hours.

The whole thing caused her insides to liquefy. The deep timbre of his voice alone was enough to set her nerve endings into spasms. Add that to the new glint in his hazel eyes and it was enough to unbalance even the most sure-footed person.

Her brain was yelling for her feet to move, but they seemed to be rooted to the floor. Every inch of skin prickled with awareness as Zane moved closer. She couldn't see him, but she could feel him. Heat seemed to radiate off his body and arc to hers.

She was now in a dangerously sensual situation. Her heart was in jeopardy, and this was just the beginning.

Her body felt alive. Every pore, every inch of flesh longed to be touched. Not in the soft, almost carefree manner it had been treated to in the past.

She wanted to be loved. Truly loved in the way that was so overwhelming neither party would be aware until completely sated.

It was scary and went against everything Serena had been taught as a young woman. Not only that, but giving herself so completely to a man like Zane meant there was no going back.

He had said as much himself. His words played like a broken record over and over in her mind.

You'll be mine. One hundred and ten percent all mine. I won't settle for anything less.

"Rena," he whispered in her ear as he came up behind her, making her shiver.

A near breathless whimper escaped her lips as she felt his warm, muscular body so close to hers. He was already hard. The feel of his length pressed into her lower back was extraordinary.

Then bending at the knees, he slowly tilted his hips forward snuggling his raging erection firmly within her cleft causing her body to tremble.

The sensation of him pressed so intimately to her along with his tantalizing masculine scent nearly brought her to her knees.

Snaking an arm around her waist, Zane expertly began to remove her belt. She stood like a statue, unable to move, to think. The only thing Serena was capable of at the moment was to feel what Zane was doing to her. To experience the multitude of sensations his every touch produced.

His fingers moved with slow and steady perfection, which she thought to be very unfair considering she was having such a hard time not sliding to the floor in a helpless heap, until her wraparound dress came fully open, top to bottom, exposing her already peaked nipples. Her breasts felt heavy with desire. Desire she struggled to fight although she had no idea why.

Serena lowered her chin until she could watch Zane's large hands as they moved to just beneath the swell of her breasts. One wicked finger from each hand moved in sync around and around her areola never quite touching her aching nipples.

As the sensations grew, Serena wiggled into Zane's groin. *Maybe if I tempt him,* she thought silently, *he will cease with the torture and get down to business.* She soon learned that wasn't the case as Zane's hips lurched forward. She was now pressed so tightly against the counter she couldn't move even if she wanted to.

Of course, that didn't stop her from trying.

"Stay still," Zane huskily whispered as he nipped her earlobe. His actions caused her to shiver earning her another nip.

"Zane." She couldn't think. Did his name actually make it out of her mouth? She couldn't be sure. Nothing was clear except for the need churning deep within her.

With her hands braced on the counter, Serena arched her back. It was pure instinct and need. The need to get closer to those hands. To drive him to the edge so he would give her what she wanted.

When he still didn't move his hands to cover her breasts or touch her in any way differently, she whimpered, "Zane?"

"Be still, baby," he answered in a soothing tone.

She could feel her blood begin to boil. The need to climax was overwhelming making her edgy. Before Zane finished murmuring in her ear, Serena tried to turn in his arms, shaking her head all the while.

Instead of allowing the movement, Zane pinned her arms to her side and leaned in to her until she could only pant with anticipation.

"Don't tell me no, Rena. Tell me what you want. Ask for what you need. Talk to me, but please don't ever tell me no. It makes me crazy, baby."

He said it softly. His tone was once again soothing, but lined with just an edge of steel. She knew he meant the words, but she wanted to deny him. To deny the hold she'd permitted him over her body, her heart. She couldn't do it though, all she could do was accept him as he was. Accept her body and its needs.

"All right. But please…" she began then abruptly stopped when two very skilled fingers began rolling her already taut nipples.

"Please what?"

"Oh, god, Zane. Please…please let me come." The words were torn from her lips as she felt the swipe of his tongue along the outer shell of her ear.

Then she felt him move. The pressure of his hand, fingers spread wide, remained at the small of her back, but the warmth of his body was gone, missed.

Soon her dress was pulled from her shoulders leaving her in only the cream-colored lingerie she'd bought just for him. Before she could move, his hand was once again splayed across her lower back. It pressed just enough to let her know he wanted her to stay, but her body wouldn't listen.

As soon as his hand was gone, Serena tried to turn and reach for him. Her body inflamed with her need to join with his. To feel the length of his cock gripped tightly within her depths.

Her movements earned her a stinging smack on the fleshy part of her right ass cheek.

"Ouch!" she gasped reaching for the hot, tingling spot on her derriere.

"I warned you not to move, Rena. Now stay still and you'll get what you want. Move again and you'll get something completely different."

Zane moved his hand ever so gently over the patch of flesh now marred with his print.

She shouldn't have liked that. She assured herself she didn't, but there was no denying the wetness between her thighs. The sting was now just warmth. More heat added to the inferno already bubbling in her almost sending her up in flames.

* * * * *

Zane knelt behind Serena and smiled against the back of her thigh as she went completely still. She was a fast learner. He wasn't so sure that was a good thing.

He kissed his way up one leg, then down the other, stopping here and there to explore. He paid special attention to every place that brought sweet sounds from Serena's lips. He could smell her arousal and longed to taste her heat, but it wasn't time yet.

Tonight he would explore her body in a way he'd never dreamed she'd allow. Every swell, every dip, every newly discovered part would be his to taste, to touch.

Very gently and very slowly, so as to draw out the torture, Zane lowered the shorts of her lingerie set. Once the garment was around her ankles, he lifted first one foot, then the other until she was free from its confines. He then tapped the inside of her knee.

"Spread those sweet thighs for me, Rena."

Obediently, she responded. Ever so slowly, his hand traced up the inside of her leg, stopping just short of the place he was sure she wanted him to touch most.

Soon he would give her just what she wanted. Her anticipation would make it so much better for both of them.

As his hand slid gently from the inside of one thigh to the other, she began making low moaning sounds in the back of her throat. He could tell she fought the urge to move as he cupped her wet sex. His middle finger slightly pressed her clit as his teeth grazed her ass.

The combination of sensations must have been just right because she bucked her hips forward searching for the release he relentlessly held away from her.

He knew the moment she realized what she'd done because she stilled mid-thrust. Being the ever-consistent man he was, Zane delivered a stinging smack to the opposite cheek at the same time he thrust a finger deep inside her wet channel. He thought he heard her gasp *oh shit*, but couldn't be sure.

Backing his finger out, he added another to it and returned them deep inside her warm reservoir, making little "come here" motions, in search of that sensitive bundle of nerves. His tongue snaked out to lick and taste the bounty of his labors. She was delicious, like warm honey.

He was sure his actions didn't remove the sting from her flesh. If anything, it brought more blood flowing to the area, which sent her over the edge. Her body shuddered just as he felt her inner muscles clench his probing fingers. She was hotter and wetter than he'd ever seen her before. And this was just the beginning.

Waiting until she could hold herself up, he removed his fingers from her dripping sex. Then slowly he slid his way back up the length of her body.

Her head hung forward, her hair covering her face. Next time he would watch her climax. Next time she would watch while he made her come over and over again.

But for now, he would hold her. Soothe her. He was curious what her reaction would be to his treatment of her. When she regained her composure would she be angry? He couldn't be sure what she would do.

Every message her body sent him told just how much those two stinging slaps turned her on, but would her mind cause her to balk at such treatment? They would have to talk about it. Discuss her feelings and work through them until they were both satisfied.

The heat on the palm of his hand was a reminder of just how much the pink flush of her bottom had turned him on. The little yelp she'd given at the time of the first slap made him a bit wary, but when she didn't ask him to stop, he had to wonder. The wetness of her swollen cleft told a story of its own.

The scent of her arousal, musky and sweet, almost sent him over the edge. He hadn't been so hard in years. Hell, he'd almost shot his load right in his pants at the taste of her and he'd never even made it to the best part.

He gathered Serena in his arms and headed for their bedroom. The night was young. The lessons just beginning. He would taste her cream. Lap every bit of it up until she begged for mercy. Then he would start all over again.

And when the time was right—when he could no longer hold back, he would sink his length into Serena's sweet depths. The first time would be fast and furious. His engorged cock was beyond ready to pound into her over and over until they were both sated.

After that, he would bathe her and prepare her all over again for a slow and sensuous journey from which there would be no return.

Upon entering the room, Zane laid Serena on the bed. Her eyes were open, staring straight at him. A beautiful flush moved from her neck up. The color reminded Zane of the pink handprints he'd left on her delectable ass cheeks, he groaned.

Grabbing her hands, he slowly pulled until she was sitting up. He couldn't help himself so he leaned forward until their lips met. She was warm and smooth and tasted like bliss.

His tongue traced the seam of her mouth until her lips parted. Beyond thought, Zane let loose. His tongue delved deep as he devoured her mouth. When he finally regained control and pulled away they were both panting.

Serena's wide-eyed stare made it impossible to go slow. There was no fighting the urge to take. It was primal, instinctual. He had to have her. Mark her as his, dominate and control. Later would be the time for slow loving.

"Hold your arms up."

She arched a questioning brow, but did as asked.

"You won't be needing this," he said as he removed her camisole over her head as if he were undressing a child. But that's where all parent-like behavior came to a crashing halt.

On the way down, his massive hands closed over two rounded breasts. When her back arched, he lightly pinched both nipples, she immediately stilled. If he wasn't so damned hard he might have smiled, but as it was it took every ounce of control not to mount her like a wild animal.

"Lay back, baby. Stretch your hands way up high and grab the headboard. Don't let go until I tell you to."

Her already wide eyes went just a fraction wider. Their green depth flashed just before the color deepened to that of moss. Her pupils were dilated. She looked like a wild, wanton creature with her hair flowing free around the pale skin of her shoulders.

He was sure she was going to argue, but she must have thought better. After the slightest hesitation, she lay back. Her lids lowered and her arms extended making her breasts lift in offering.

"Open your eyes. I want you to watch everything I do to you. I want to see your soul through those pretty green eyes when you shatter."

His words made her squirm. She tried to press her legs together, but he was too fast. With his body stretched over her, his hips nestled snugly between hers there was nowhere to go. Unless she let go of the headboard. He watched the realization flicker briefly across her face and gave her a smug smile in return.

It was a silent challenge and she was well aware of it. He could tell she had decided not to push him—at least not this time. If he knew his Serena at all though, he knew it wouldn't take her long to test the limits he'd set for her. He was looking forward to the day.

When Serena stilled, Zane lowered his head to a rose-tipped nipple. Lightly flicking it with his tongue while grinding his shaft into her, he brought her back to the peak. All the while never taking his eyes from hers.

Just when she showed every sign of falling over the edge, he pulled back. He moved slowly, deliberately until he was standing at the foot of the bed.

Serena raised her head, spearing him with her gaze. He watched as her eyes followed the motion of his hands as they removed his shirt. Sitting, he proceeded to take off both shoes and socks, then stood and cupped his hard length through the fabric of his pants.

The tip of her pink tongue peeked out to moisten her kiss-swollen lips. Her hair was fanned against his pillow. His eyes roamed lower until they met with the glistening peak of her nipple still moist with his saliva.

His fingers fumbled with the catch of his pants. He wanted her so much he felt crazy with it. As he knelt on the bed between her still spread thighs she made as if to move her hands.

"Stay just the way you are, Rena," he warned.

"Zane. Oh, Zane, I want to touch you."

"Not yet, baby. One touch from you and it's all over. I can't wait, Rena. I can't wait. I'll make it up to you." Before the words had completely left his mouth, he was on her. In her.

Slow, deep thrusts brought him closer by the minute. Lifting Serena's legs until they were wrapped tightly around him, he thrust into her causing her to cry out.

He prayed she wouldn't ask him to stop, he wasn't sure he would be able to. Never had he used her so fiercely, but there was no stopping, no slowing down.

"Oh, god, Zane," she panted. "I need...I need..." Her words trailed off as his teeth tugged at one pebbled nipple.

"Come with me, Rena." Once, twice, on the third stroke he felt his body stiffen. He came with a force he'd never before experienced. Serena cried his name, her body convulsed around his softening cock. In exhaustion, his spent, sweat-dampened body collapsed against her.

A few hours later, Zane awoke to Serena's warm body snuggled in close next to him. Her hair, loose and wild was flowing about her shoulders all but begging for his fingers to tunnel through it.

His cock was hard and ready but he wouldn't take her as he had before. This time would be slow and torturous for the both of them. Slipping silently from the bed, Zane made his way to the living room where he collected the nondescript brown paper bag he'd set on the end table upon returning home.

With bag in tow, Zane made his way back up the hall and into the bedroom where he set the bag on the nightstand before going into the connecting bathroom. He took out a small ceramic washbasin and filled it with warm water. A fluffy washcloth was the only other item he would need. After dropping the washcloth into the water-filled basin, Zane carefully made his way back into the bedroom anticipating what was to come.

"Rena," Zane said, his voice low and soothing. "Wake up, baby," he added when she only snuggled deeper.

When Serena finally turned onto her back, Zane crawled onto the bed beside her. He was rigidly aroused but it would have to wait. He had plans for Serena that took precedence over his cock.

As quietly as possible, he pulled the blue vibrator and dildo from the bag then set them beside where she lay on the bed. With his hands, he spread her thighs wide running his fingers up and down their silky length. His touch caused Serena's eyes to flutter open. For a moment, she looked a bit confused but Zane knew right away when she'd come fully awake because her cheeks turned the prettiest shade of pink.

"What are you doing?" she asked, her voice low and soft.

Zane wrung out the dripping washcloth then proceeded to lay it over her mound. "Just taking care of what's mine."

"Mmm, that feels wonderful." The more she spoke in her low, almost purring voice, the harder his cock got.

When Zane felt he'd sufficiently cleansed and soothed Serena's pussy, he set the blue vibrator on its lowest setting and ran it in circles around her clit basking in her moans and cries of pleasure. His ever-decreasing circles came close but never quite touched the tiny bundle of nerves now swollen with arousal.

She was wet. He could see her juices glistening on her labia even in the dim light spilling from the slightly opened bathroom door. With slow yet sure movements, Zane introduced the lifelike dildo he'd bought into Serena's sex, watching as she opened for its invasion.

Her body bucked beneath his hands trying to get closer to the buzzing of the vibrator even while her hips moved urging the dildo deeper. She was hot. This time he did nothing to stifle her movements. He merely watched in awe as her body took over, its need consuming her.

When Zane felt that he'd sufficiently tortured them both with his sensual play, he removed the dildo from her tight sheath, its surface covered with her juices. Zane handed the vibrator to Serena as he moved to his knees between her still spread thighs. With his hands on her hips, he tugged until her bottom was elevated and in perfect alignment with his cock then placed her feet flat on his chest.

With one hand under her, cupping her bottom and the other grasping his throbbing shaft, Zane invaded Serena inch-by-inch fighting to keep control as he did so. With his now free hand, Zane urged Serena to pleasure herself with the still buzzing vibrator.

Within moments of doing so, Zane could feel the tiny tremors of her pussy as his body built towards its climax. When it hit, Serena's body grew taut mere seconds before clasping his cock. Her body held him so tightly he had no choice but to follow with an orgasm of his own. Even afterward, he could feel the tiny spasms that continued to rack Serena's body and knew that the position he was in was right where he always wanted to be.

After regaining his breath, Zane removed the toys and the washbasin to the bathroom leaving behind only the paper bag. It still held a few items Zane was sure would come in handy at a later date.

Zane climbed back into bed and pulled Serena to him spoon fashion. He lifted her leg until it rested on his thigh then worked his already hard shaft back into her still wet pussy.

"Zane?" she asked drowsily.

"Shh, it's okay. I just need to feel you, baby. I'm not sure I'll ever get enough of you," he said then buried his nose in her hair. Her soft sigh was like music to his ears as he drifted off to sleep.

Chapter Eight

ॐ

The next few weeks flew by in a blur of activity. Sometimes it seemed as if her life had been flipped upside down. So much change in such a short amount of time made her head whirl.

And yet, some things in her life hadn't changed at all. She still worked hard doing a job she loved. Only soon, she would be doing it from Texas.

Zane was keeping longer hours preparing for the move. Even while working such hours in preparation to move his business, he never neglected what Serena considered to be her lessons.

She smiled at the thought. Often over the past few weeks, she'd pushed Zane. Just enough to see what she could get away with. It amazed her just how much she was willing to trust him. How easy it was to give herself to him over and over again, night after night.

At first, she worried about following through with this new sensual side to their relationship. Would Zane ask too much from her? Would he not ask enough, leaving her wanting and needing more? Would her needs bring back memories of her ex, a relationship better left in the past?

Now she knew the answer to all the questions pounding through her head.

He may push but he'd never ask for more than I'm willing to give, she realized. A small shiver went up her spine. Never had she been left wanting unless it was what she considered to be part of the learning experience.

She recognized it early on. Like a kid in a candy store, she wanted to gorge on everything in sight only to be left with a bellyache. Zane had insisted on patience. Sometimes he was as hard-pressed as she was to hold out. To let the passion build until it could no longer be held. In those instances, she would writhe and plead for him to finish with her. To give her the release her body so desperately needed.

Then there were the times where she wanted to wring his neck. He always held so tightly to his control. Even when he was so hot and hard he could do no less than take her with deep, hard, animalistic thrusts, he was still in control.

To think that he could accomplish such control while she screamed with the intensity of her release made her see red.

No matter how hard she tried, his wicked tongue, nimble fingers and engorged cock were always too much.

She longed to see him deep in the throes of passion. To see him lose his control. It would happen very soon, even if she had to push a bit more than she was comfortable pushing to get him there.

Going into this type of relationship was new. She was well aware they wouldn't always agree, but this new side of him, the autocratic side he'd never shown before, was sometimes very hard to deal with, Serena thought, as she felt her smile turn to a frown.

Thinking back to last night, Serena followed their discussion from beginning to end through her mind and was still in shock over the outcome.

Her nipples peaked and goose bumps skittered across her skin in response.

He'd walked through the door to her office at half past seven last night. It had been a rough day and the medication she'd taken for the thrumming in her head was wearing off.

She sat bent over her keyboard typing furiously trying to ignore the fact that someone else was in the room. If she could just get the rest of the information saved before she lost her train of thought, she would be finished for the night. But that wasn't to happen evidently.

"Rena," he said as he kissed the side of her neck, which was stiff with stress.

"Just a minute, Zane," she answered not aware of the curtness in her voice.

It had taken no more words. Zane reached over her, pressing the appropriate keys to save her work while holding her hands still. When she'd turned to him, furious at the interruption, he'd silenced her with a harsh kiss.

"It's late, Serena. You can finish tomorrow."

She narrowed her eyes at him. "Why you...you," she sputtered completely oblivious of his growing arousal.

"Be quiet, baby," he growled.

"I will not be quiet. And you had no right to do that, dammit! I wasn't done."

She no sooner got the words out of her mouth than she found herself hauled up and out of her chair to be plastered against Zane's solid length.

One hand was tangled in her hair. She felt the pull at her scalp, but gave no consideration to it. She was angry and was spoiling for a fight. Now was as good a time as any, she remembered thinking. Then all hell had broken loose.

She felt a telling dampness between her thighs as memories paraded, one after another, through her mind.

While one large hand had held her head immobile, the other cupped her denim-clad backside pressing her close. He ground his hips into hers making it impossible to ignore the bulge beneath his zipper.

Just about the time she was ready to give in—to melt against him, he said, "I want you ready when I come home, Serena. That's why I called earlier, to let you know I was on my way." His voice was gruff, commanding and the use of her full name let her know he meant business.

She wanted to rant and rave, but every time she opened her mouth, he silenced her. Finally, she freed her mouth from his. Placing her hands flat against his chest, she pushed. The rock-hard wall of his chest was warm under her palm, but it didn't budge an inch. All she managed was to arch her upper body away from him. In the process, she brought their lower bodies impossibly closer together.

Serena gasped as Zane once again began to lower his head.

"Zane, wait!" Something in her voice must have alerted him. His head stilled mid-swoop.

Nervously, she smoothed her hands against the shirt stretched tight over his chest and tried not to breathe too deeply of his mesmerizing scent.

When he finally loosened his hold, she continued. "You said you'd listen to me, Zane. But every time I try to talk you kiss me."

She could tell he was struggling not to laugh. The darned man was infuriating!

His full lips quirked up at one side. "Go ahead, baby. I'm listening," he crooned.

Now that she had his full attention, she couldn't think of what she'd wanted to say. His loose hold in no way masked his arousal or allowed her freedom. The burgeoning length of him was hard to miss at any distance.

Heat flashed behind his cool façade making her hunger for what he had to offer.

Serena buried her face in his chest inhaling deeply. It did nothing to help clear her head of wayward thoughts.

His fingers grasped her chin and tilted it up until her eyes met his.

"Say what you want to say, Rena. If you keep rubbing up against me like that, I'll take you right here on your desk."

He was getting impatient. She could tell by the tenseness of his jaw, the way his hands flexed and relaxed against her body.

Good, make him wait. She'd given in to his every whim over the past few weeks, it wouldn't hurt him to wait just a little bit.

You may have given in to his every whim, her mind taunted, *but you've received pleasure back tenfold.*

His arm tightened around her as his head slowly lowered. He stopped when his mouth was just a breath away from hers causing her skin to prickle with awareness.

"You're running out of time," he said as his palm kneaded her backside.

"Please, Zane. I can't think when you hold me this close," she said pulling away from him, giving a silent prayer of thanks that he'd let her go. She paced away, placing the entire length of the room between them. It was purely a defense mechanism. She needed room to breathe, to think. To be out of Zane's grasp and to keep her senses clear until she said what she needed to say.

"I know you called, but I lost track of time."

Running her fingers through her hair, she sighed.

"It's been a long day and it seems like nothing's gone right. Then, you just waltz right up and shut my computer down like what I do doesn't matter."

She was getting angry all over again. The blood was pumping in her veins making the pounding in her head more pronounced. There was little she could do to stop it.

* * * * *

Agitation showed in every movement she made. From the rigid set of her shoulders to the furrow between her daintily tweezed brows. Her white-knuckled hands were fisted and resting on the swell of her hips, which were cocked sassily to one side, foot tapping a fast-paced staccato.

She was royally pissed and beyond gorgeous. The flush high on her cheeks, pouty kiss-swelled lips and the flash of her emerald eyes made her look like a wanton goddess. Damn but he wanted to sit her on the smooth surface of the desk and settle himself between her thighs.

Serena in a snit was a glorious sight to behold. No longer could he hold back so he started for her. Slow and steady, he made his way across the room. He watched as warily, Serena took several small steps in retreat. When she could go no further, she started moving to the side.

Zane had the hardest time containing the laugh eager to burst forth. He was curious as to where she thought she was going. Casually, as if he had no care in the world, he stopped his forward progress.

Serena's eyes narrowed. She was waiting. He could see the wheels spinning, trying to figure out what his next move would be. When he moved away from her, in the direction of the door, she made to move back to the chair at her desk. But when the lock clicked into place, she froze. She was so still, he wasn't sure she was even breathing.

Once again, he moved toward her. "I said I'd listen and I did. I never said a thing about agreeing though, which I don't," he said as he advanced upon her.

"This is our time, Rena. Time to learn what we thought we knew. I won't have work getting in the way of our future whether it's your work or mine. The sooner you learn that, the easier it'll be."

He thought steam would soon be flowing from her ears as red as her face was. Her body nearly vibrated with anger. About the time he finished his little speech, she made a beeline for the door.

This time he did chuckle, he couldn't help himself. Her antics were nothing less than entertaining. Upon hearing his laugh, Serena turned on him and advanced, completely forgetting her need to flee the room.

Her small finger poked his chest in time with her words.

"I-don't-care-what-you-think," she enunciated slowly as if he were slow in the head all the while poking his chest with a manicured nail. He wasn't quite sure if he wanted to laugh or paddle her ass. Her next words made his decision.

"I'm going to finish my work now. If you're so damned hard up you can't wait until I'm done, then go fuck yourself!"

A deep, rumbling bark of laughter filled the room. He'd never seen the little hellion so pissed. This was exactly what he'd been waiting for. A legitimate reason to get his hands on that cute little ass of hers.

He held out a hand to her, raising an eyebrow when she didn't comply with his silent demand. He could sense her confusion—it made his lust stronger.

His shaft twitched with the strength of his arousal. He wanted her to fight him. To kick and scream, first with uncertainty tinged with fear and later from sheer pleasure. A pleasure almost as hot as her bottom would soon be.

"Don't make me come for you, baby. I can't guarantee you'll like the outcome," he threatened in an ominously quiet voice.

She backed further away from him. "Zane?"

He circled his wary prey. Once around her, he leaned against the still locked door and crossed his arms over his chest. All outward appearances showed him to be in complete control. Loose-limbed and relaxed from head to toe. Only he knew the truth.

He was hotter than a schoolboy making a play for his first score. Silently, he hoped with everything in him that she didn't call his bluff. He wanted her to come to him of her own free will.

He was one hundred percent sure she wouldn't enjoy herself right off, but everything he'd learned of her in the past few weeks told him she would absolutely love the heat and arousal she'd gain in the semi-forced scenario he planned to see through.

Giving Serena a brief respite, he remained leaning against the door trying to force every ounce of concentration from within his lust-filled brain, trying to retain his composure. Slowly, he willed every muscle in his body to relax. Every muscle obeyed the silent command except for the important one. The one tenting his trousers in defiant erectness.

Once again, he held out his hand and once again, she backed away. It was quite comical and he might have laughed if his senses weren't on such high alert. There was no way the sassy-mouthed vixen was going to get away from him.

"Serena, baby. If I come get you, you'll be over my knee so fast it won't be enjoyable for either of us."

He watched as her mouth fell open, revealing pearly white teeth and a pink tongue. It almost immediately snapped closed.

"Enjoyable," she sputtered.

"Yes, enjoyable. Can you already feel it, Rena?" he asked in a near whisper as he closed the distance between them.

He kept her eyes glued to his, willing her to move toward him. His eyes bore into hers; he saw her shiver and knew he had her complete attention.

"I bet you're already wet for me, baby. Just anticipating my hand on your ass is making you hot."

Her head was shaking side to side. He interrupted before she had the chance to start protesting.

"Don't tell me no," he growled reminding her of his earlier warning. "And don't lie to me. You're so hot those luscious nipples of yours are already pouting at me."

By the time he finished, he was close enough to test his theory. With the pad of his thumb, he grazed her left nipple through her clothes, wringing a gasp from deep inside her.

As his hand threaded through her hair, he was reminded of the softest silk. She was smooth all over. Inside and out. His penis dripped pre-cum at the thought of being buried within her silky depths. His mouth watered at her remembered taste.

Sweet and musky, all woman and sensual as hell. The thought of feeling her smooth buttocks against his palm brought forth a rumbling groan.

Nostrils flared, Zane tugged her head back at the same time his free arm locked her body to his.

"I can smell your heat," he said inhaling deeply. Leaning forward, he blew warm air into the curve where her neck and shoulder met feeling tiny bumps on her skin raise in response.

Then with a long, slow swipe of his tongue, he licked the lobe of her ear just above where his breath mingled with her scent. She melted in his arms causing him to grasp her even tighter.

She was right where he wanted her. Relaxed and aroused, now to get rid of her clothes.

As his mouth plundered hers, taking everything she gave and more, he lowered the zipper of her jeans, then worked them over the swell of her hips until they pooled at her feet.

Thankfully, there were no pantyhose to contend with and the tiny triangle that was her panties did little to detain him. Soon they joined her jeans, around her ankles on the floor.

She was so caught up in their scorching kiss and the fingers rolling her nipple, she showed no sign that she realized he had just undressed her from the waist down.

She tasted of citrus and sunshine. The warm sounds she made as his tongue traced her lower lip damned near made him forget what he was doing. His body begged him to take her swiftly, but he had other plans.

With both hands, he held her head still for the pursuit of his mouth. She wiggled against him trying to get closer, to ride the thigh he'd just wedged between her legs.

He slowed the heated kiss until it was tender, yet thorough. He heard her sigh with contentment when one hand traveled the length of her spine until it reached the swell of her bottom where he squeezed once before a resounding slap filled the room.

When she cried out hands flying to cover her stinging parts, he let her go and slowly moved to the chair at her desk where he then sat.

"Take off your shirt and bra, baby. Then come here so we can do this the right way."

"Zane?" she panted, hands still moving behind her.

He watched as Serena lifted first one foot and then the other, removing her jeans and panties from their tangled position around her ankles so that she could walk to him unencumbered.

"Now, Rena," he said in a tone new to her. One that brooked no argument. Combined with the predatory look he knew was plastered across his face and he was sure she was wondering just what in the hell she'd gotten herself into.

Chapter Nine
ဢ

She could feel her body tremble. She quivered with need, fear of the unknown and an arousal so deep she wasn't sure she'd ever be able to wade herself out of its depths.

When he stood from his seated position on her desk chair, her feet involuntarily gave a little hop. *So much for showing only outward calm*, she thought wryly when one brow lifted in response to her jerky movement.

Mesmerizing, that was what he was. She couldn't have torn her eyes from his fluid movements to save her life. So, she stood like a stone statue and watched.

She watched as he removed a square box from the pocket of his sport coat and set it beside her keyboard on the smooth surface of the desk. His tie, which already hung loosely at his throat, was removed next. When his deft fingers pushed first one button and then the next through their respective holes, her insides protested. The shiver running down her spine only made her weakness more pronounced, at least to herself.

His movements caused the air around him to stir and when he finally removed his coat the rich aroma of musk and male monopolized her senses.

With each flick of his wrist, his sleeve inched higher until it was neatly rolled, just under the elbow. Her eyes were still glued to his every movement. Serena watched as Zane rolled the opposite sleeve noticing how the movement caused the muscles in his forearms to contract and relax.

It had seemed like hours, but in reality must have only been minutes. However long it was, it hadn't been long enough before he once again resumed his seat. This time he chose a ladder-back chair.

She was still trying to understand why he would choose the most uncomfortable chair in the room when he cleared his throat. Too soon, she was once again aware of exactly what he expected of her.

Did she dare deny him? Did she want to? The answer to both questions was a quick no.

Not just no, but hell no!

Serena stifled a nervous chuckle and tried to concentrate. It was so hard to do with him sitting as big as you please at the side of her desk. Arms bared and large hands resting on thighs she knew for a fact were strong and corded with lean muscle.

Thighs she was supposed to drape herself across for her first-ever, honest-to-goodness spanking. Damn if that thought didn't make her wet.

She was once again brought out of her reverie when Zane said, "Serena dear, you pushed, now it's time to pay."

She could tell he was getting impatient. His eyes may have been glittered with lust and there was definitely a flush of arousal high on his cheeks, but his voice was edged with steel and his hands no longer sat idly on his thighs.

Taking a deep breath, she blindly moved forward. With every tiny step, she reminded herself that this was exactly what she'd been looking for. Precisely what she wanted.

She was so hot the scent of her arousal wafted up filling her senses until she thought she'd burst. So turned on she was sure her juices would be coating her inner thighs before she ever made it to him.

Her mound throbbed with each shuffled step, squeezing her thighs together did nothing to ease the mounting tension coiled low in her belly.

It was an odd feeling to walk across a room bared from the waist down while your man sat patiently—or in this case, not so patiently—by and waited for you to arrange yourself across his lap to feel the sting of his palm against your backside.

Would the bite of pain be as wonderful as she'd imagined it would be? Would the resulting heat radiate through her body and make her all but beg to be taken? These were questions she couldn't wait to have answered.

When Serena finally reached the spot just before Zane's seat, she stopped and waited. And wondered. The quirk of his lips made her a bit uneasy. It was a mischievous smile. One, that knocked her a bit off-kilter making her vulnerable and uneasy. These feelings in turn made her defensive, possibly even a bit angry.

She tried to remain calm, but when he motioned with a finger for her to turn around, all thought ceased to exist, melting her anger away in the process.

This was it. It was time. Stiffening in anticipation, she felt the muscles in her bare bottom clench. When the touch finally came, it wasn't at all what she'd expected.

A warm hand ran the length of her spine from the cleft of her butt to where her bra was still fastened. It was then that she remembered. He'd told her to remove her shirt and bra and she hadn't done it.

Damn, damn and double damn! She berated herself. Sure, she'd wanted to push him. To see if he would follow through with the erotic promises of a spanking if she didn't comply with his every whim.

Hell, she'd spent the past week sashaying around the place like a bitch in heat trying to get him to lose the control he held to as tight as an old spinster held on to her virginity. And now she'd done it. Only this time she thought there was a chance she may have gone just a smidge too far.

"I asked you to remove these, baby," he said as his fingers worked the clasp of her bra.

She tried to turn in order to face him. She desperately wanted to make amends, to show that she would comply. That she wanted to experience his loving hand, but she couldn't seem to gather her thoughts enough to form a few words much less a sentence.

His hands at her hips held her firmly, not allowing her to turn or step away. And when she finally forced enough brain cells together to speak, she was stopped by his next words.

"Now, turn around and remove your shirt and bra, Rena. We'll add a bit extra to make up for this little discrepancy," he said as she turned in his hands head dipping forward. The open-mouthed kiss he placed just below her navel once again caused her brain cells to scatter.

The bat-sized flutters tearing their way through her stomach combined with the trembling of her hands and the moist, warmth of his mouth moving along her heated flesh and Serena wasn't so sure she'd ever get her shirt off.

When she finally managed to release the last button, she sighed in relief. Next came the cream-colored lace bra, which already hung loose. When both were pooled at her feet, she straightened her shoulders, lifted her head and once again waited.

The kisses peppering her abdomen and the large hands firmly grasping her thighs made her head spin. Without thought, she leaned into Zane. Hot need kindled deep inside.

His throaty chuckle as he eased her away snapped her back to attention.

"Not yet, baby. Not for a while, we've got other business to attend to."

His voice was smooth and deep and although her body and mind felt torn, it soothed her.

"Place yourself over my lap, sweet thing. I want that ass of yours right where I can reach it."

"That's a girl," he crooned when she lowered herself until her belly rested on his thighs.

Serena could feel the blush of embarrassment as his hand moved over the bare skin of her bottom. Zane shifted beneath her, spreading his thighs, allowing her more room. Making her more comfortable — if that were possible. One thing became crystal-clear just after she moved to shift her weight.

With his legs held wide the way they were, her clit was finally getting the attention it had been demanding. This revelation caused her to squirm even more.

"Uh-uh," tsked Zane. "Not yet," he said as he held her steady with a strong arm across her lower back.

"Now I want you to hold on to the chair the best you can, and keep those sweet hands of yours out of my way or I'll tie them."

When she complied, he gently stroked a hand up the inside of one thigh and down the inside of the other. "Open your legs, baby. I wouldn't want to miss anything."

She couldn't help the shiver that ran the length of her body. Oh, god, she inwardly moaned. She shouldn't like this. She shouldn't want to be tied and spanked, but she did.

And for once, coming to that conclusion didn't leave her feeling dirty or deranged. It left her hot and so damned horny if he didn't get on with it already, she'd find herself in even bigger trouble.

The sting of the first smack was much lighter than expected. It wasn't harsh or hard and neither were the several that followed causing her skin to tingle. Soon though, the heat began to build. Serena fought to stay still, but as each subsequent blow landed, her pussy was ground into his leg bringing her higher and higher until she was sure the next would send her into orbit.

* * * * *

His hand was on fire. He could only imagine what her ass felt like. It was hot and almost the same color pink as he knew her nipples to be after they'd been sucked vigorously. His cock was rock-hard and he wasn't sure he'd be able to wait much longer.

He'd started off peppering the twin-rounded globes, gradually graduating to her upper thighs. A couple of throaty moans escaped her lips causing him to slow a bit. Lust tore at him. Take, his body demanded, but he couldn't take the chance that he'd hurt her so he slowed and waited. Waited to hear if she panted the safe word. Would he be able to let her go if she did?

She was so wet. He could see the lips of her pussy glistening with the moisture of her arousal. He could feel her heat. When she seemed to calm down, but didn't utter a word, he continued. This time his hand lifted and lowered much slower, but each strike was harder than those he'd started with. Her body quivered under his arm. He could feel her hips move as she tried to grind her clit against his leg.

When her movements became frantic, she panted out his name.

He had to know.

"You okay, baby?"

"Y-yes," she breathed out, nodding her head at the same time.

"That was for not being ready when I got home. This is for defying me too many times to count since then."

The sound of the next three swats rang out clearly into the quietness of the room along with her voice.

"Ohhh," she cried as the sound of flesh on flesh once again filled the air. When he knew she was ready, he ceased his movements instead running a finger along the cleft separating her magnificent ass and ever so slightly grazed the one spot on her body he'd never praised.

Lowering a finger until it reached her drenched sex, he collected the moisture found there and returned to the spot between her cheeks.

Teasing and testing, he gradually added pressure until his finger breached the last of her body's virginity. She gasped and moaned.

That was all it took, bucking under the pressure of his finger, she cried out his name. He could feel the tight muscles of her anus grasping the tip of his finger and knew he'd die of bliss when he was finally able to take her there.

With a hand between her legs, covering her mound, he turned her tucking her close to his chest until the spasms of her orgasm eased.

Her breath came in short gasping pants. Zane could feel the sheen of moisture covering her body. When she wiggled to get closer, his shaft throbbed in protest.

Her lips, now roaming his neck, only made matters worse. It was as if his body had been taken over. The caged animal had been let loose and would never again agree to such confinement.

He could only hope she'd understand, he thought, as he stood and carried her to their room.

After laying Serena on the bed, Zane removed his clothes. During that time, she'd lifted herself up on to her elbows and was watching him. Her gaze was intense. Green eyes stared at him as though seeing him for the first time. When he opened the top drawer of his bedside table and removed a length of black silk, those green eyes widened. The depth of color and dilated pupils made him want to roar with triumph.

Instead, he motioned her to him. When she was stationed on her knees on the bed, he moved forward. His large hands cupped her elbow pulling her close for a heated kiss.

His mouth devoured hers, nipping at her full lower lip, sucking it between his lips when she gasped. Lifting her against his chest, he stepped away from the bed then slowly lowered her down the length of his body until her feet touched the floor.

Zane watched as Serena's head titled just the slightest bit to the side. She wanted to question him, he was sure, but had yet to open her luscious lips.

He raised a single finger to his mouth in a gesture for her to remain silent. Her eyes immediately sparked in response. The glittering emerald of her irises remained locked to his face as he gently turned her until she faced away from him.

Caressing her ass with his right hand, he asked, "How do you feel, baby?"

She turned her head his way looking at him over her shoulder. Raising one arched brow, she challenged him. He could almost hear her wheels spinning. Why had he told her to keep quiet to then ask her a question?

When she remained silent, he patted her ass and nipped the back of her neck. "Good girl, Rena."

She stiffened at his words, but the hand roaming her still tender flesh must have given her pause, still she didn't speak.

He chuckled as he gently but firmly added pressure to her shoulder until she took the hint and slowly dropped to her knees.

"Cross your hands behind your back," he commanded in a voice low and sensual.

When she followed his orders, he wrapped her wrists in the length of silk, firmly but gently binding her. Now to turn the fantasy he'd so often masturbated to into a reality.

Chapter Ten

&

The carpet abraded her knees, but not to the point of discomfort. Her senses were reeling. Every smell, every sound was magnified. She could almost taste his heat, his utter maleness. Her mouth watered in response.

The strength of the black silk binding her wrists was surprising. The thin fabric was silky smooth. The length left hanging skimmed the heated flesh of her bottom causing an overabundance of already heightened nerve endings to protest. Or beg, Serena wasn't sure which.

She seemed to tingle all over after Zane securely bound her wrists together. The feel of his warm hands grazing her body ever so slightly while insisting she stay still and quiet, made her want to scream.

Now she was at his mercy. His every command would be hers to follow or pay the consequences. Sitting back on her haunches, Serena watched as Zane silently left the room, closing the door behind him.

Every emotion imaginable ran through her mind at that point in time. But the one prevailing emotion that took precedence over all others was trust. Her trust in Zane was unequivocal. Just as her love was all consuming.

Damn, there it was again, she thought as her shoulders slumped and her head fell forward. She loved him. There was no denying it, and no longer could she hold it back.

She was so lost in the magnitude of her feelings that she didn't hear when the bedroom door opened to admit a nude Zane.

Nor did she see the frown upon his face as he noticed her stooped shoulders, her look of defeat. The frown marring his polished good looks was one of concern.

"Rena baby, what's wrong? Did I...? Do you...?" He didn't finish, voice trailing off as his hazel eyes stared into hers.

The concern in his eyes brought tears to her own. Tears she tried desperately to blink away, to no avail. This was a turning point for them, a new beginning. She wasn't supposed to be blubbering like a baby.

One hand rested on her shoulder while the other tilted her chin up.

"Oh, god, Rena," he started only to be interrupted.

"No, Zane, don't," she said softly wishing her hands were free so she could smooth his furrowed brow. To cup his face in her hands and kiss him tenderly.

"I'm... It's just that..." Damn, they made a good pair. Couldn't get a full sentence out between the two of them. Taking a deep breath, Serena swallowed then tried again.

"It's just that I love you, Zane O'Malley. With all my heart and soul, I love you." There, it was finally out. There would be no taking the words back. Not that she wanted to.

The waiting would kill her, she was sure. He said nothing in return, just stared. His eyes bore holes into her soul and yet, he remained silent.

She felt as if she were choking. Swallowing past the lump lodged in her throat was virtually impossible. Until she saw stars dance before her eyes, she didn't realize she'd been holding her breath. It came out in a whoosh.

With its release also came the tears. They snaked like twin rivers down her cheeks and she was powerless to stop them. Serena closed her eyes and dropped her head. The rasp of a warm finger across her wet cheek was the first move Zane made since she'd spilled her guts.

He pulled her close, kissing the tears from her eyes, from her cheeks. He uttered words she couldn't understand as he stroked her hair away from her face.

In his intense gaze, Serena saw everything. Love and passions like she'd never before witnessed. She could feel the smile as it slowly but cautiously spread across her face. Zane's eyes sparkled at her in return.

"I've never heard words more beautiful. With all my heart and all that I am know that I love you, Serena Keller," he said as he continued to kiss her face.

"Also know that from this day forward you will belong to no one but me."

With those spoken words, Zane picked up the square box Serena hadn't even noticed sitting on the bed. Next to it was a plain brown bag. She had no time to consider what might be inside of it because at that very moment, Zane opened the velvet jeweler's box.

Inside laid a gold choker. The intricate pattern looked ancient. Set flush into the gold was tiny emeralds sparkling as if winking at her.

Serena gasped and struggled with the silk still holding her wrists captive. Zane's chuckle brought her gaze back to his. Her breath hissed out at the sight. He was bent on one knee in front of her. His shaft proudly erect, curving slightly toward his abdomen. On his face, he wore a look so possessive, so primal Serena could only stare mutely in return.

"We'll just leave you like you are, baby. I'm not done with you yet."

With those softly spoken words, Zane clasped the gold choker around Serena's neck then stood to his full height bringing his penis in direct line with her mouth.

Serena couldn't help but lick her lips in response. His scent wrapped itself around her like strong arms in the night. Taking all she had to give while making every moment special.

She leaned into his embrace, a bit unsteady without her hands. Leaving everything to Zane, she sighed when she felt his fingers tangle in her hair bringing her forward until the smooth head of his shaft was pressed to her mouth.

She snaked her tongue out until the tip peeked from between her lips and stroked him ever so slightly 'round and 'round the sensitive bulb of his cock head. When his hips bucked, she smiled.

Sitting lower against her heels put her in the perfect position to tease and tantalize. With soft strokes, she licked him from base to tip, then paid homage to his swollen testicles. It was hard to balance with her hands bound, but Zane helped guide her.

Taking one completely into her mouth, she sucked and then released.

Soon her head was grasped firmly from both sides. Her hair moved away from her face, then she heard the growled command. Or was it a plea?

"Look at me, Rena. I'll watch you take me. And when I come, I'll feel your eyes on me as well as your mouth."

The words alone wrung tiny orgasmic spasms from her already taut body. With her eyes fastened on his, Serena took him completely in.

* * * * *

The feel of her hot, little mouth surrounding his cock while the depths of her green eyes stayed trained on his face was almost too much. It took what was left of his willpower not to plunge his length to the back of her throat.

Her hair was wrapped around his fingers. The amber highlights against the skin of his tanned hand was such a turn-on. When his hands tightened, tugging her closer, she lost her balance. The tiny whimper of need that escaped her throat when his length was dislodged from her greedy lips caused his mouth to tilt at the corners.

She raised an impatient brow at his blunder then resumed where she'd left off. The swelling of his cock was a fair warning causing his toes to curl. When she pulled him to the back of her throat then stroked him with swallowing motions he was lost.

Balls tight against the base of his shaft, Zane's seed spewed forth, all but erupting from his body. A strangled cry burst from his mouth and filled the room while grass green eyes watched, never leaving his face as she swallowed all his body offered.

Spent and hardly able to stay upright, Zane collected Serena into his arms. His woman, his submissive woman, the woman who not only let him spank her, but also tie her and fuck her mouth. When she was sitting comfortably on the bed with a smug smile drifting across her face, Zane leaned in to remove the length of silk still binding her wrists.

When her arms were free, she moaned softly.

Zane turned Serena onto her stomach. When she was lying flat, he straddled her hips and began to massage her shoulders and arms.

Rena's lean muscles were tight beneath his palms. Zane continued over her upper body until he felt her relax. When he was finished, he made his way down her neck and back, nibbling, kissing and licking a direct path down her spine.

It shouldn't have been possible, but the sweet sounds and the rolling of her hips made it so. His flaccid cock sprang to life once again. He didn't think he'd ever get enough of their new relationship. Of this new Serena, his Rena.

Slowly, languidly, Zane continued the path he was on until his tongue was darting over the curves of her ass. Using his shoulders, he spread her thighs wide. Blindly reaching out, he snagged a plump pillow pulling it beneath her. Once Serena was settled onto the pillow, Zane strategically placed her sex where it was most convenient for him and his voyage.

With thighs opened wide and hips raised, Serena would be the one doing all the writhing and moaning this time around.

Zane slowly kissed his way up her inner thigh. When he reached the apex, he stopped and inhaled deeply. Her scent was all woman. She was sexy as hell with her ass in the air, open and ready for all he had to offer.

A chuckle escaped his lips and she wriggled trying to get closer to his mouth. With both hands, he tortured and tormented her dripping sex, keeping her teetering on the edge.

His breath fanned over her wringing a moan from deep inside her body. When she was frantic in her search for release, he buried his face between her thighs, dipping his tongue deep within the warm recess of her body.

Licking and lapping, he brought her closer and closer, yet refused to send her over. She tasted like honey, sweet and smooth on his tongue. He told her so, the words dark and erotic causing her breath to hitch, then pour out of her lungs.

"Oh, god, Zane. I love it when you talk to me like that."

He could feel the tiny spasms of her imminent release on his tongue. Now was the time. Time to make her fly. Dipping his head lower, Zane deftly licked at the swollen nub of her clit while his roaming hands worked the cheeks of her ass teasing the cleft parting them so he could reach all her hidden treasures.

"Hand me that bag, baby."

"Bag?" she asked looking back at him over her shoulder. Her face flushed, her eyes glazed.

Pointing to the brown bag, Zane continued with his foray through her folds. Although he had slowed down, he knew Serena was impossibly close to her release. He intended to make it an unforgettable one.

"What's in it?" she asked.

"Just turn around and relax, baby. You'll love this, I promise."

Dumping everything out of the bag, he found the anal toy he'd bought. It was a smaller size for beginners and would be perfect for Serena. Generously lubing the toy, he caressed her cheeks while completely letting up on his tongue torture. She groaned in response.

"Don't stop! Please don't stop." Her voice was gruff, her breathing ragged as she moved her arms as if to lever herself up from her awkward position perched atop the overstuffed pillow.

"Stay there, Rena. I'm not going to stop, baby. Not until you've come so many times your body has no more to offer."

His words made her shiver causing chill bumps to immediately spring to life all over the surface of her skin.

When the toy was slick enough, he took the bottle of lube and prepared her body. Her moans of pleasure and gasps of pain were beyond arousing as he prepared her tight, virgin entrance with the width of his finger. Her body clenched tightly as he slowly reversed his motion. A feminine moan slipped from her lips, her body shuddered.

"You okay, baby?"

"Oh, yeah," she answered, her body screaming for its release.

Slowly, he worked the toy into her tight hole. Breeching the ring of muscle caused her to still, her breath to hiss out with every breath. The widest point wrung a whimper. Its fully seated width and length got a groan.

Zane gave the toy a slow twist before rising to his knees. Below him, Serena's back heaved with the effort to breathe. Her smooth skin was covered with a glistening sheen of perspiration making it seem almost glittery.

Her position was perfect for his entrance. With slow determined thrusts, he entered the cream-covered length of her cunt. Her already tight sheath was made impossibly tighter by the toy lodged deeply within her anus.

"Zane!" she screamed as her climax overtook her body.

At the very moment her voice filled the room, he thrust full and deep, imbedding himself completely within her.

"Damn, baby. This is so good. You're so good," he groaned mindless with arousal.

Leaning forward, he nipped her neck, tasting her sweet skin. He could feel the base of the toy against his pelvis and gave a small thrust stimulating not only the fist-tight length of her cunt with his deeply buried cock, but simultaneously her nether hole.

The sensation must have been overwhelming because she was thrown immediately into another orgasm. This one was all consuming, causing not only her inner muscles to spasm but her whole body seemed to go rigid with the intensity causing his own release. It was just as emotionally and physically earth shattering for him as he imagined it was for her.

When her body relaxed with only small tremors of her release remaining, Zane pulled her into him and held her close. Held her tight.

"Rena," he whispered into the darkness later that evening.

"Hmmm?" she replied drowsily as she changed positions, turning her body to face him.

Fingering the gold choker clasped around her neck, he said. "You have this, but it's not enough, baby. I want you to wear my ring."

She peered at him in the darkness of the room then blinked. It did nothing to remove the confused look from her face.

When she said nothing, he sat up. Once he'd turned on the small lamp on his bedside table, he turned to her.

"Your ring?" she squeaked.

"I'm asking you to be my wife, baby. Will you do that for me? Will you wear my collar and my ring?"

He watched as tears spilled over onto pale cheeks. She was shaking her head no, but her mouth said yes.

"Yes," she repeated still fighting her tears.

"Don't cry, Rena."

"Oh, god, Zane. I love you!"

She was in his arms in a flash. Her enthusiasm tumbling them backward onto the mattress. He held her to him, over him so that he could see her face.

"Everything is almost ready for the move. I want to get married at home, in Texas, with my brothers close by. How do you feel about that?"

She hesitated for a moment before answering. "What if your family doesn't like me, Zane? What then?"

He kissed her forehead, a big smile on his face. "They'll love you, baby. Just as I do. I've already told them I was coming home and they're ecstatic. Last night before I came home, I called and left a message telling them I was bringing you with me. I'm expecting a return call first thing in the morning, knowing my brothers."

As he'd expected, early the next morning, the shrill ring of the phone seemed to scream through the room. With fumbling hands, Zane reached for his alarm to shut it off before realizing it was the phone. With a grumble and a few choice words, he picked up the cordless phone and punched the talk button.

"What?" he groused.

A deep chuckle met his ears. "Wake up, baby brother," the voice said.

"Dammit, Sean! Do you know what time it is?" Zane asked as he swung his legs over the side of the bed, his hand scratching his bare chest.

"Yep, sure do. It's morning. What, do people in California sleep the morning away."

When they've been up all night making love they do, Zane thought silently as he looked over his shoulder where Serena had curled onto her side and was softly snoring.

A smile crossed his lips when he answered. "There is a two-hour time difference, you moron."

"Oh, sorry. I didn't think about that one," Sean answered not sounding the least bit contrite. "You going to tell us what's going on, Zane?" This time he sounded worried.

"I'm coming home for good, Sean, and I'm bringing Serena with me."

A slow whistle sounded on the other end of the phone. "Why now, Zane? Why after all these years?"

Without going into specifics, Zane told Sean how he'd placed a singles ad and Serena had answered it.

"Well, I'll be damned!" Sean managed to get out between hoots of laughter.

"Sean, I've asked her to be my wife and I want to be married at home. I've talked to Hayden about staying at the ranch until we buy our own place." Just saying it made it seem so real. He was finally going home for good.

"Are you sure about this, Zane? I mean, these damned women are enough to drive a man crazy."

Hostility from Sean was not a good thing. He may seem like a big ole teddy bear, but the man could be downright scary when he wanted to be.

"What women, Sean?" The other end of the line remained silent. "Spill it already. I don't have time for this crap."

A whoosh of air was the first sound he heard since asking the question.

"Do you remember Honor Rollings, Zane?"

"Vaguely," he answered not at all sure where this conversation was going. "Wasn't she that scrawny kid who came to live with her aunt?"

"Yeah, that's her, only she's not scrawny anymore and she's definitely not a kid. She's back. The widow Rollings passed away a few weeks back and she came home to get things in order."

Zane scratched his head, then ran a hand over his face. Serena had turned toward him and was now curled up around his hips while he sat at the edge of the bed. Her closeness was making his cock as hard as a fence post, leaving him with little patience.

"Tell me all of it, Sean and do it quick because I've got to go."

A deep chuckle once again sounded in his ear. Then it was gone, to be replaced by a sobering voice.

"She's working for me waiting tables. Seems she's been traveling from place to place all these years. She's never settled down."

The edge in this brother's voice had him a bit worried. "Some people are just like that, Sean. What is it to you if she doesn't stay put for long?"

"Because she's mine!" Sean answered in a possessive growl. "She doesn't know it yet, Zane, but she's mine. I fell in love with her the moment she walked into my place and I won't let her go. I can't."

"What did you do, big brother? Tell her you want a house load of kids and scare her away? You know some women don't want that."

His brother was a big man. Intimidating. But he had a heart of gold and since the time Zane could remember, he talked of marriage and family.

"No, I didn't quite make it that far. I told her she belonged to me and if I caught her with another man I'd beat him to a pulp and paddle her ass until she couldn't sit."

Zane's laughter woke Serena. Her tiny hand snaked around his hip until it rested low on his abdomen making his semi-rigid shaft throb in anticipation.

"From your tone, I'm assuming your words didn't sit too well with her."

Serena mumbled some appreciative words along his right hip as her fingers walked their way to the thatch of hair surrounding his now proudly erect penis.

"So, Zane, is that her I hear? And why all of a sudden has your breathing turned ragged?" Sean teased.

"Can it, Sean. I've got to go. I'll see you in about a week," he groaned then promptly hung up the phone.

In one swift motion, he was poised over Serena. He nibbled once on her ear and in an agonizing breath whispered, "Sorry, baby. I can't wait, I'll make it up to you, I promise."

The words were no sooner out of his mouth than he thrust himself into her. This was no gentle loving session. It was raw, untamed sex. The sounds of flesh on flesh filled the room until his head spun and he came with the ferocity of the animal he felt within himself.

Serena's cunt gripped him tightly; tiny spasming flutters were all that remained of her orgasm when he finally roused himself enough to remove his weight from her body.

The rest of the day was spent doing exactly as he'd promised—making it up to her for his fierce lust and lack of finesse. He accomplished that by playing with her until he though they'd both go insane. Then with bodies entwined, they slept.

HONORING SEAN

&

Chapter One
ℵ

Light filtered through the dimly lit room as the front door opened. Of its own accord, the slab of heavy oak snapped shut behind the woman who'd just entered through it. To the hulking man standing next to the bar, the room suddenly seemed brighter as if a shot of pure sunshine had found its way through the thick brick walls.

The tall, lithe figure of Honor Rollings moved further into the room, astounding him. It still amazed him how easily she had accomplished, in the blink of an eye, to steal his heart right from his chest.

Her jerky movements indicated her anger level, and damn, but she was cute when she was mad. He couldn't help the rumbling chuckle that escaped his lips.

"Mornin', Little Darlin'," he said by way of greeting.

His "Little Darlin'" who wasn't so little by today's standards, stalked right up to him, toe to toe, thighs to knees, nose to chest.

He pegged her at about five eight, but to his six-foot-three-inch build, she may as well be a fairy. With her hands fisted on her slender hips and her blonde hair billowing like a cloud around her shoulders, she looked like every healthy American man's idea of a wet dream.

Her clear blue eyes burned with righteous indignation.

"Don't you *Little Darlin'* me, you...you...big oaf," she all but snarled, as she stomped one dainty sandal-clad foot in her fit of rage.

His face hurt from trying to hide the grin begging to break loose. Her head was thrown back allowing her to see his face without forcing her to back up. The woman had courage, he'd give her that much. There weren't many people willing to stand toe-to-toe with Sean O'Malley.

Of course, the tempting view he had of the delicate arch of her neck was causing him some problems. Combined with her scent, and the rapid rise and fall of her pert little breasts as she ranted and raved, and he was a goner.

The monster in his pants was stirring, insisting on its fair share of attention, but in actuality, all that was being accomplished was to make the fit of his jeans uncomfortably tight.

"Are you listening to me, Mr. O'Malley?" she asked, punctuating the question with a manicured nail to his chest. "I can't believe you did that. You had no right!"

Grabbing her under the elbows, he lifted her off her feet until she was eye to eye with him.

"Now that's where you're wrong. I had every right. I warned you, Little Darlin'. Warned you the minute I saw you and recognized you as mine what would happen."

He watched as her eyes narrowed to slits. Ice blue and cold, they probably scared most men with their intensity.

"Oh, for the love of God, would you put me down?"

When he returned her safely to her feet, she just continued to stare up into his face. "Mr. —"

"Sean, I told you to call me Sean. Dammit, Honor, there are many things I'll allow, but you and other men isn't one of them, so don't ask it of me.

"I did just what I said I'd do under the circumstances. Well, almost all of what I'd said. We'll take care of the rest later, don't doubt it."

Just as he finished speaking, the front door opened, allowing entrance to a small group of people. It was just before dinnertime on a Thursday night. Handing a white apron to Honor, Sean made his way back behind the bar to continue stocking the refrigerator with bottled beer.

When she leaned over the bar, giving him a birds-eye view down the scoop neck of her silky peach blouse, he looked up.

"We're not done talking Mr. O'Malley," she hissed between clenched teeth. "I don't know where you came up with the scatterbrained idea that I belong to you. I've only worked for you for three days. I can tell you though, that who I see is none of your business. I do not belong to you now, nor will I in the future. As soon as I have a bit of cash in my pocket, I'll be out of your hair."

This time Sean couldn't hold back the booming laugh or the wide grin that spread itself across his face. Running one hand over his smoothly shaven head, all he said was "We'll see, Honor, we'll see."

* * * * *

Shaking her head, Honor stalked to the booth in the corner while wrapping the white apron snugly around her waist. *The man was an ogre*, she fumed silently.

Once she'd served drinks to the four people seated at the booth, Honor went back to her silent fit of pique. Never in her life had anyone made her want to curse more than Sean O'Malley did.

It was one of her personal goals in life, to never stoop to using foul words as part of her everyday language. Not only that, but the fact that her father The Major would have had some seriously stern words to say to his daughter had he ever heard her utter a foul word, kept her on the straight and narrow.

She liked being ladylike. Dressing neatly and keeping her language clean was only a small part of it, but the danged man behind the bar made it nearly impossible. And now, for some off-the-wall reason, he thought she belonged to him.

She couldn't help the shiver that raced down her spine at the thought. He was more man than she'd ever before encountered. Even her own father who she'd thought had hung the moon, couldn't measure up in size.

There was just something about the man that insisted upon being shown respect. The commanding way he carried himself and the deep baritone of his voice only added to his overall appeal.

She tried to keep the thoughts of last night far from her mind's eye because when she thought about the whole incident, she wanted to kick something.

Humiliation was a hard thing to swallow, but the knowing looks and nervous giggles had been too much.

It had all been in fun. Never in a million years did Honor think Sean would follow through with his threat. As a matter of fact, until he'd shown up last night, she'd even forgotten the argument ever took place. Evidently, Sean didn't forget as easily.

Now though, the ominous words spoken during the short argument on the day they'd once again met played through her mind. His parting words that day had made her blush.

You belong to me, Honor. If I catch you with another man, I'll beat him to a pulp, and when I'm done with him, I'll paddle your ass until you can't sit.

The man must be stark raving mad! Sean may have met her briefly as a teenager, but when he'd voiced those words, she'd known him as an adult for less than twenty-four hours. Weren't men supposed to be commitment-shy? Why did she have to pick a place of employment where her employer stated within minutes of meeting her that she was the one. It was asinine.

And at the same time, it made her very curious. She'd only lived in Texas with her aunt for two years before feeling the need to travel. Those two years had been some of the hardest of her life. Growing up as an only child to a loving older couple who thought they'd never have children had been great, but their simultaneous deaths in a car accident on her sixteenth birthday had changed her life forever.

It was something she tried hard not to let get her down. Something she preferred not to talk or think about, and the reason she still didn't celebrate her birthday.

Even though her time in Texas had been short, she remembered vividly the gossip about the wild O'Malley brothers. Silently, she wondered where the other two were.

Moving from place to place was in her blood. It was the way she'd grown up, the only way she knew. It was also what she'd argued with Sean about. The way he saw things, she'd been claimed and that meant she'd be staying, with him, for the long haul.

She was so caught up in her thoughts that she didn't hear him come up behind her until his brawny arm clamped around her waist, drawing her closer to his body. When her back was pressed firmly to his chest, a massive hand settled possessively along her abdomen.

Warmth from his body flowed straight into hers, pooling at the needy place between her clenched thighs. When his breath rasped along her ear, she thought her knees might buckle.

"Don't think so hard on it, Little Darlin'. It'll all come out right in the end, you'll see."

Her initial reaction was to kick him in the shin, but the finger playing lightly along the outer swell of her breast in combination with the warm lips traveling along her neck and the swell of his arousal pressed against her lower back brought all thought to a screeching halt.

"I don't understand you, Sean O'Malley."

Honor opened her mouth to say more, then decided not to. In some ways, the man standing behind her was a big teddy bear, all soft and cuddly. In other ways, she feared he was as immovable as a mountain range. Something deep inside her warned that she was one subject he wouldn't be changing his mind about.

As an independent woman, used to doing as she pleased, when she pleased, she wasn't sure exactly how that made her feel.

When the front door once again opened, Honor tried to pry herself loose of Sean's grasp.

"Not so fast there," he said before turning her to face him. "You understand me, Honor. You just feel the need to fight it, but that's okay because where you're concerned, I'm willing to be patient as long as you don't overstep the bounds I've set for you."

Just when she thought he was being sweet, he turned back into a Neanderthal.

"Mr. O'Malley. You, sir, are an exasperating man." She felt her anger rise and was afraid if she let loose she'd do something to embarrass herself even further, so she turned on her heel to walk away, only to be brought up short by a firm, but gentle grip on her elbow.

"Little Darlin', you're pushing awfully hard. I already owe you one, now it won't bother me none to add to it, but I can't guarantee you'll like it."

With a quick flick of his wrist, a slightly stinging blow landed on the swell of her right butt cheek.

She felt her eyes widen at the same time her jaw dropped. Both hands automatically moved to cover the site, rubbing the newly heated area.

"Now run along and take care of those customers, Little Darlin'. Or you could call me Mr. O'Malley again and we'll settle up right now."

Her feet couldn't move fast enough. The nerve of the man was astounding. He couldn't possibly be serious, could he? The lingering warmth radiating across her derriere proved he was. It also made her thighs tingle and her panties wet. *This couldn't possibly be normal*, she thought to herself, fighting the blush she was sure was riding high on her cheeks.

She'd read about men who enjoyed that type of thing, but she'd never personally encountered one. For all she knew, it could be a Texas thing. Maybe men in Texas thought they had the right to spank their women in order to keep them in line. The problem there was that she wasn't Sean's woman.

She hadn't been a virgin for years, but she wasn't promiscuous. Her partners were chosen carefully, she was very picky when it came to the men who would grace her bed. Due to that little quirk, she had very little actual experience. The fact that she would normally pick out a man the complete opposite of Sean O'Malley worried her a bit. He seemed so rough around the edges, so uninhibited compared to the staid business types she normally kept as company.

Did it really make a difference? Would he really be so different? With every ounce of her being, Honor knew the answer to that was yes.

Remembering the night before set that answer in stone within her mind. One minute she'd been happily dancing with a man who seemed like a nice gentleman and the next, she'd been hauled up against what felt like a brick wall with one steely arm around her waist while the matching arm of the brick wall smashed in the nose of her dancing partner, sending him sprawling to the floor.

Just thinking about it made her spitting mad all over again, which wasn't a good thing since she had seven hours left in her eight-hour shift.

Chapter Two
ဢ

Sean couldn't help but smile as he watched Honor once again take the long way around the room in order to stay as far away from him as possible.

Her lissome form seemed to float across the floor. The three-quarter length of her coffee-brown drawstring pants left her bare from mid-calf down, showing off a hint of golden tanned legs. The leather straps of her sandals hardly seemed enough to hold the shoes in place, allowing pink-tipped toes to wiggle freely. And although her breasts were small, they were perky. What more could a man ask for of his soon-to-be-wife?

Curiously, he wondered if she'd liked the love tap he'd bestowed on her fine ass. He sure as hell hoped it was something she would learn to love because the surprise on her face, as well as the way she'd rubbed the sting he'd left, had brought his cock to life, leaving him hard and ready.

Now, he couldn't concentrate on a thing. All he was able to think about was her ass. Her skin would be smooth and warm. It would start out milky white and by the time he was done peppering the fleshy globes with the flat of his hand it would be berry pink, just the way he liked it, the same color he imagined her nipples would be.

Of course, he didn't want to scare her away, and never in a million years did he want to hurt her. It was more a matter of showing her a different side of him, and in the process, teaching her a lesson she wouldn't soon forget.

He watched as Honor made her way around the room, from table to table. Her smile was dazzling, and it seemed the little vixen got along with everyone, women and men alike.

It was the men who made him jumpy. The way their eyes followed his woman around the room made his baser instincts roar to life. He wanted to snatch her up and haul her away from them all, but instead, he watched and waited.

He could tell more and more just how much Honor was aware of him. It seemed that as the night grew later, her fight to keep him out of her mind waned. Soon she began stealing peeks when she thought he wasn't looking. The big mirror behind the bar was good for keeping an eye out when his back was turned to the room at large.

Rubbing his hand across his face, scratching a finger through his neatly trimmed brown mustache in the process, he thought of something else the mirror behind the bar would be good for. Those thoughts made a fantasy jump right to the forefront of his mind.

Before, the woman had never had a face, but now her wanton blue eyes and fair blonde hair stood out in his mind. She'd sit proudly, but shyly on the cool, smooth surface of the bar doing what Sean asked. He often dreamt how the woman would spread her thighs wide when prompted to do so. She'd watch herself in the overlarge mirror as Sean played with her. And when she climaxed, spilling her juices across the wooden surface beneath her, he'd bend low, burying his face between her thighs, tasting of her until she begged for mercy. All the while, she'd watch in the mirror.

Shaking such thoughts from his mind wasn't an easy task, but what was happening in the room behind him gave him no choice.

Honor was strutting her stuff across the floor blatantly flirting with each and every man she came across. The sway of her hips had gone from gentle to sassy, and the smile that lit her face up was nothing short of mischievous.

His emotions warred through him. He wanted to wring her neck and lay out every man in the room who so much as looked her way. At the same time, he thought of how much fun it was going to be when he finally had her across his lap. The palm of his hand itched to get on with it.

As he continued to watch, Honor's gaze swung to where he was standing with his arms crossed over his chest. He met her gaze with a warning one of his own. Instead of looking properly chastised, the damned woman smiled and winked then continued on about her merry way.

Oh, yeah, it was going to be a long night. A long, good night filled with wickedly erotic happenings when he finally got Honor Rollings behind closed doors. The monster in his pants could hardly wait.

* * * * *

The blasted man was going to be the death of her. There was no way she couldn't have noticed how his eyes continued to follow her.

He just watched her, blatantly, out in the open, possessive attention. It was unnerving in a sensual sort of way. Of course, if he didn't knock it off soon, she was going to have to change her panties. Staying dry around this wet-dream-of-a-man was virtually impossible, and it made her angry that he could manage to keep her off balance so easily.

At first, she'd tried with all her might to ignore him, not giving him the time of day unless it was to order drinks or drop off empties. As the night wore on though, ignoring Sean proved to be virtually impossible. His shirt was stretched way too tight across the bulging muscles of his chest and upper arms. His faded button-fly jeans hugged him in an obscenely sexual way. Faded white in all the right spots, a ragged tear along one knee exposed just a bit of skin. Seeing that tiny bit of flesh made her mouth water. The fact that she wanted to run her tongue along it should have warned Honor just how far gone she already was. The very large set of polished Redwing boots adorning his feet only added to his overall sex appeal. He was a hard man not to drool over.

She'd made darned sure to keep far away from him because once he set his hands on her, she wasn't sure what would happen. She would either jump his bones or kick him, and it wouldn't be very professional to do either during business hours. So, she'd done her best to keep focused on the task at hand. Smiling when appropriate, talking when a customer started a conversation.

Twice already, she'd turned down offers to dance. After last night, there was no way she would be responsible for another broken nose.

About the time that thought came to mind, Honor felt the tiny hairs on the back of her neck rise. It had to be him again.

Slowly she turned, and what she saw left her a bit shaken. The broad expanse of his shoulders was facing the room, but his face could clearly be seen in the mirror behind the bar.

His eyes seemed darker than normal and feral, a sense of foreboding shivered across her flesh. His hooded gaze seemed to be trained on her, and yet, he seemed to be staring right through her.

Man, he could make her insides quake without so much as a how-do-you-do and it made her want to scream.

A naughty little thought came to mind. One the little devil riding on her shoulder just wouldn't let her push away. Adding a little extra sway to her hips as she made her rounds around the room gave her a feeling of feminine power.

The extra wide smiles of the men she served as she leaned in close sent a tingle of anticipation down her spine.

The big brute behind the bar may be able to stomp one dancing partner into the ground with a single punch, but it was very unlikely he would or could take on a whole roomful of men. So, she set out to flirt with each and every one.

Deep down, Honor was aware that she was pushing Sean O'Malley beyond his limits, but something in her just wouldn't allow her to back down.

When the hair on the back of her neck once again stood at attention, she turned her gaze to the bar, gave her best I-am-woman smile and winked. The look of barely leashed anger he returned was a warning she chose to ignore. The second of sheer confusion she witnessed just as she'd winked would make it all worthwhile. With a shiver of excitement and a chuckle, she continued her way around the room.

After taking a large order, Honor made her way to the bar. Once she'd finished relaying her order to Sean, with a promise to be right back, she turned to leave, needing a quick bathroom break, but Sean had different plans for her.

Grabbing her wrist in an unbreakable hold, he bent low and all but growled at her. "What in the hell do you think you're doing?" His breath smelled of mint. Honor couldn't keep her eyes off his mustache, loving the way it moved when he talked.

"What do you mean what am I doing? I'm doing my job," she said, while trying to pry her wrist loose of his grasp.

"Dammit, Darlin', I'm trying mighty hard to stay in control here, but the way you keep sashaying that tight little ass of yours around this room full of men is driving me crazy, so knock it off."

When she opened her mouth with a retort, she was cut off by a hard, smacking kiss. Sean's huge hands were now holding her head as he looked deeply into her eyes. The intensity of his gaze brought a volley of shivers running up and down her spine.

"You may still be fighting it, Honor, but mark my words, you will be mine, so don't go offering what no longer belongs to you. I'm just about at the end of my tether, Little Darlin', and my hand is just itching for the feel of your backside."

Stepping away from the large man still holding her, Honor said, "There you go again! Would you just stop it? I've already told you, I don't belong to you." Then, as she turned to walk away, she added, "And if you think I'll let you lay a hand on my behind, you're crazier than I thought, Sean O'Malley."

As she made her way the ladies' room, she couldn't help but admit that the idea of being spanked by Sean O'Malley was as equally frightening as it was arousing.

Later that night, Honor wondered if it was worth it. Her feet were killing her and she had aches in muscles she wasn't even aware existed. From the bulge of her apron pockets she would have to assume she'd made a killing in tips though. All that hip swaying and smiling had been good for something at least.

It sure hadn't earned her any extra attention from the boss man. After that one look of warning and the heated words they'd exchanged, he'd gone about business as usual. Funny how that bothered her, but it did.

After drying the last of the glasses, she set them on a rack at the end of the bar then made her way to the back room for her personal belongings.

Once finished, she headed back up the hallway. The door to Sean's office was open so she stuck her head in to bid him goodbye.

"I'll see you tomorrow," she said quietly to the man working behind the desk.

"All done?"

"Yes, I just finished the last of the glasses."

"Hold on there. I'll walk you out."

Honor couldn't help but wonder what he was up to. He seemed way too calm for her peace of mind.

"Umm, okay, but you don't have to," she said, hoping he'd decide to stay.

"I'm done here," was all he gave in the way of an answer before meeting her at the door.

They walked side by side down the hall until they reached the front door.

Once outside, Honor gave her thanks to Sean and hurried off to her car. *I'm not running away*, she argued silently with herself, knowing full well it was a lie. It was just that something about Sean's cool demeanor left her feeling a bit jittery.

For some off-the-wall reason Honor realized that a broodingly quiet Sean O'Malley was a very dangerous thing.

She watched out her rearview mirror as she pulled out of the parking lot, breathing a sigh of relief that he'd let her go so easily after the stunt she'd pulled.

As she repeatedly reminded herself that she belonged to no one but herself, she wondered what it would be like to give herself wholeheartedly to him. Once she crossed the line though, there would be no going back, and she wasn't absolutely sure she could handle that.

Honor pulled her car up to the curb in front of the small apartment complex where she was temporarily living. It wasn't the best of places, but it was quiet and clean, and her neighbors seemed friendly enough. Also, it was the only place she could find willing to rent to her without signing a lease.

Lost in her thoughts, she didn't notice the black pickup truck that parked just around the corner, or the overly large man who slid from behind the wheel.

Juggling her backpack-style purse, Honor searched for her keys. Once found, she opened the door to her small apartment, but when she went to close the door, a hand stopped its progress.

"What the—" she started.

"Well hello there, Little Darlin'," Sean taunted, as he waited to see if she'd invite him in. When she backed up, a look of shock on her face, he walked through the door, closing it behind him.

"Wha—" Clearing her throat she tried again. "What did you need?"

The crooked smile curving his lips was purely evil in a wickedly sexual way. It made her inner core flood with feeling, her skin heat. And at that moment, she knew there was no way she would be able to turn him away.

"This, sweetheart. This is what I need," he growled, as he pulled her into his arms, up against the wide expanse of his muscular chest. The feel of wash-softened cotton and muscle beneath her palm started a tingling sensation that traveled up both arms.

His kiss came at the perfect moment because Honor wasn't sure she would be able to hold back the whimper begging to break free of her throat. Instead, the feeling was replaced by a purr of pure satisfaction as his lips met hers, and his moist tongue delved deep.

When his lips finally released hers, she was lightheaded and dazed. Before she knew what was happening, she felt the room tilt. With no time to even utter a word in protest, she found herself belly-down across Sean's lap.

"We've got some catching up to do, baby," he said, as his hand rubbed across her backside. "I told you I owed you one, and now it's time to accept payment. This time you can keep these cute little pants on, but the next time it'll be bare skin I feel beneath my hand."

The first blow to land on the fleshy part of her bottom made her jump. It wasn't exactly comfortable, but not quite painful either.

Several more landed leaving her feeling as though her bottom was on fire. She couldn't help but wiggle and squirm as she was held snugly across the bulging muscles of his trunk-sized thighs.

And that's when she noticed it. All the wiggling and squirming was bringing her great pleasure, the slight pain of the blows landing across her backside only made her move more until she was grinding her hips into the warmth of Sean's legs beneath her like a wanton woman.

She couldn't seem to help herself, she was so close. A low moan was wrung from her gasping lips as a firm swat landed against the bottom curve of her cheeks, pushing her up until her clit rasped against the seam of her pants.

"Oh, God. Please…please," she begged, not knowing what she was begging for.

His hand was now rubbing her hot bottom through the fabric of her pants. "Please what, baby?" he asked.

She couldn't answer. She didn't know what words to use to explain what she needed without sounding like a slut.

"Tell me, Honor," Sean commanded, rubbing and squeezing her while running a hand between her thighs every now and then. It was just enough to make her crazy.

"I need… Oh, God, Sean, I need you to touch me." Saying the words were difficult, causing Honor to duck her head in embarrassment even as she squirmed to bring her mound closer to his touch.

"Where do you need for me to touch you? Be specific, Honor, tell me exactly what you want."

She wanted to scream, that's exactly what she wanted. "Between my legs, Sean. Touch me between my legs," she panted out between suddenly dry lips, trying not to concentrate on how close she was.

"Where between your legs, sweetheart?" he asked, then grazed his fingers across the juncture where thigh met pelvis. "Right here?"

"No," she whimpered, still rubbing herself against him.

"Then tell me, Honor. I won't ask you again," he demanded, removing his hand from her body.

"My p-pussy," she stuttered through the alien word. "Please, oh, please, make me come," she all but begged.

She didn't see the smile making its way across Sean's face as he returned his hands to her. One was roaming full force between her legs, beneath the drawstring of her pants and the tiny wisp of lace covering her hidden treasure, the other hand turning her over until she was seated in his lap.

It didn't take much. A deep kiss and some direct clitoral stimulation, and she was off like a rocket, blasting into space if the stars dancing their way across her vision were any indication.

Chapter Three

ຄວ

The way she burrowed against his chest, a sigh easing from her ripe pink lips, made him feel like a man possessed, but he couldn't let go just yet. There were still things to straighten out.

She was so sweet. Her wanton movements, and the way her hair hung around her shoulders shielding her face from his view as her ass moved back and forth, had been such a turn-on. His cock was ready to go. Hard and hot, making the fit of his pants beyond tight. He could feel the dampness against the overly sensitive head of his cock where he'd leaked pre-cum with the excitement of Honor's release.

It was mind-boggling just how aroused he could get from hearing his straight-laced Honor say the word "pussy". The way she'd ducked her head while bucking her hips against his lap had also told just how much her words had turned her on as well.

From now on, he'd make damned sure she told him exactly what she wanted and where she wanted it. To hear her beg for her release, her voice thick with lust as she forced the sexy, unfamiliar words from between her lips would be so over the top he'd probably come in his pants just listening to her.

"Come on, Little Darlin'," he said, lifting her into his arms as he stood. The feel of her body against his was mind-altering. *Hell, who needed drugs when you had a willing woman like Honor Rollings in your arms?* He chuckled at the thought.

"Where are you taking me?" she asked, while running one inquisitive hand along his chest.

"To your room, sweetheart. I'm going to get you ready for bed and tuck you in." He received no answer in return.

When he reached the door to her bedroom, he opened it with one hand. *She was as light as a feather*, he thought, as he sat her on the edge of her bed.

"Sean," she breathed out as he removed her shirt. The silky fabric slid over her body with ease. Her eyes fluttered open for the briefest of seconds before once again closing. The dark crescent of her lashes in contrast to the creamy paleness of the skin just below them. The way her brows furrowed into the slightest frown told him just how relaxed she was. A sexually sated Honor was a wondrous sight to behold. She looked absolutely beautiful.

"Shhh," he whispered back as he eased the arm from out behind her, which had been holding her up, until she was laying flat.

Once that had been accomplished, he made quick work out of removing her shoes, slipping the straps of her sandals off, rubbing where they bit into her feet. Her pants came next. They were loose fitting and not hard to remove once Sean untied the drawstring waist.

Every ounce of willpower was used when he saw the tiny pink triangle covering the juncture of her thighs. Oh, how he wanted to kiss her there, to taste and tease her until she could hardly catch her breath. But it wasn't time. Not yet. For now, she needed rest, and when she was finally rested, she would have a lot to think about.

He wondered how she would act come morning. Would she be overwhelmed by all the new feelings his spanking undoubtedly released, or would she be angry? Only tomorrow would tell.

Before he gave himself any time to change his mind about staying, knowing full well what would happen if he did, he left her room after quietly turning off the light.

Back in her tiny living room, he straightened her things. Her bag was still on the floor where it had fallen when he'd gained entrance. A few items had fallen out so he picked them up and put them back into the bottomless pit she called a purse.

One of the items shocked him just a bit. It was a little rectangular package of birth control pills. He wasn't quite sure how that made him feel. On one hand, he was glad she would be ready when they finally made love, because more than anything he wanted to be embedded deep inside her warmth with no barrier between them.

On the other hand, though, he wondered why she was on the pill. Was there a man somewhere waiting on her? She'd only been back in town for a short while, taking care of things after her aunt's death. Staying had more to do with needing money than anything else, from what he understood. But if she did have a man, then why hadn't he come with her?

It was all too much to think about, and left him in a bad mood. The thought of his Honor with another man was enough to ruin even the best of days.

He could feel the scowl crossing his features, but did nothing to hinder it. There would be no other man and after they were married, she could continue to take the damned pills if she wanted, but he hoped she'd want to start a family right away.

Confused, and not in the best of moods, Sean headed home. Once there, he decided he'd return his brother Zane's call, first thing in the morning.

Zane was the youngest of the O'Malley boys and would be coming home soon. It would be great to have the three of them back together again.

With thoughts of a warm and willing Honor under him, tangled within the sheets of his bed, Sean was finally able to drift off to sleep.

The morning light brought along with it an almost uncontrollable urge to collect Honor, bring her to his home and never release her. Of course, that wasn't going to happen, but for a minute, it sounded like a fine idea.

Grimacing at his overly aroused penis, Sean swung his legs off the side of the bed and headed for the bathroom to shower.

When he finished dressing, he would give Zane a call. Get a feel as to when he would be coming home and why. His baby brother had yet to say a word as to why now, after four years of being away from home, he'd finally decided to come back.

The fact that he was bringing his live-in girlfriend Serena with him was another story in itself, because Zane, like their oldest brother Hayden, had never been the settling-down type.

Sean was just getting ready to hang up when someone finally answered the phone.

"What?" was growled into his ear.

Sean couldn't help but laugh, Zane never was one to wake up with much grace. "Wake up, baby brother."

"Dammit, Sean! Do you know what time it is?"

"Yep, sure do. It's time to get up. What, do people in California sleep the morning away?" he couldn't help but taunt, only to have Zane mumble something about a two-hour time difference.

"Oh, sorry. I didn't think about that one," Sean answered, not sounding the least bit sorry. He asked Zane what was going on then listened intently when Zane explained that he was coming home for good and bringing Serena with him. They were planning to marry in Texas, with his family and friends present.

"Well, I'll be damned!" Sean managed to get out between hoots of laughter. Then he sobered a little bit and asked, "Are you sure about this, Zane? I mean, these damned women are enough to drive a man crazy."

"What women, Sean?" The other end of the line remained silent. "Spill it already. I don't have time for this crap."

Sean didn't have to wonder why Zane had "no time for crap" just now. He could hear the drowsily mumbled voice of a woman coming from the other end of the line.

Sean went on to explain about Honor. How she'd come home after learning of her aunt's death and had stayed, needing work.

He wasn't at all amused when Zane outright laughed after being told of their first argument. He couldn't help it if he'd turned into a possessive man. He'd known from the first adult moment he'd laid eyes on Honor Rollings that she was the one, and he'd told her so.

Told her that she belonged to him, that soon she'd be his wife, the mother to his kids. So what if she had looked at him as if he were an escapee from a mental institution. She belonged to him and that was all there was to it.

"From your tone I'm assuming that didn't sit too well with her." Zane said.

"To say the least." Then hearing his brother's breath gasp through the phone line, and a sultry giggle sound not too far away, Sean couldn't help himself.

"So, Zane, is that her I hear? And why all of a sudden has your breathing turned ragged?"

"Can it, Sean. I've got to go. I'll see you in about a week," Zane said, just before the phone went dead.

His brother was coming home in a week. *Watch out Texas*, was all he could think.

* * * * *

Honor woke the next morning garbed in nothing but her bra and panties with a bladder ready to burst. Scrambling from the bed, she made her way to the restroom. Once finished, she leaned forward to study herself in the mirror.

She looked the same, but she wasn't. She wasn't sure whether to be mortified over what had happened or not. What she did know was that through the burn of the spanking Sean had administered, she'd felt an intense arousal unlike anything she could ever imagine.

Her feelings worried her a bit.

Throughout her adult life, she'd craved someone to take control, someone to take care of her, to protect her. Even when her independent womanly self fought the realization tooth and nail, her inner self knew the truth. There was no denying it, but she also couldn't bring herself to admit it.

Was she willing to stay put when all she'd known was how to live simply, moving from place to place? She was well aware that part of her constant moving was a way of running. There wasn't much she would back down or run from, but one of thing was the memories of her parents' death.

Time had helped heal the pain of their loss, but even after all these years, their death still caused her heart to ache. Now, as an adult, Honor knew that she wasn't directly responsible for their deaths the way she'd thought early on. And although the realization eased the ache, it was still something she preferred not to think about, wouldn't allow herself to dwell on. Honor had a feeling that the recent loss of her aunt would make this year a bit harder to cope with.

The anniversary of her parents' death was the only time of the year Honor let go. It was the only way she could make it through the day. Usually she would wake up and from the first eye-opening moment of the day, she'd drink.

Then she'd drink some more until she couldn't think. The next two days would be pure torturous hell, but by the time her hangover was gone and she felt like living again, the momentous day had passed, and she'd have a full year until she was forced to relive it again. Right or wrong, it was her way of coping, one that seemed to work for the most part.

Unfortunately, by doing so, she was allowing a part of herself to be lost because since the day of the accident, she had not celebrated a birthday. It was also much easier to keep to herself if she didn't stay in one place for too long. Never allowing herself the closeness of a one-on-one relationship was the easiest way Honor could think of to keep herself from future pain. What was left of her family had died with her aunt. The recent loss had been hard enough, but Honor wasn't so sure she could survive losing a lover or a spouse, which was why she was so stubborn about remaining alone. That stubbornness was the reason she found herself arguing so often with Sean O'Malley.

Pushing such morose thoughts from her mind, Honor decided to instead think of the overwhelming feelings Sean had fondled from her body just the night before.

Before she could get too deeply into those intensely erotic memories, the phone rang.

"Hello," she said, answering the phone, trying not to sound breathless.

"Good mornin', Little Darlin'," the voice drawled in her ear.

"Good morning, Sean."

"How'd you sleep?"

"Fine, just fine. Thanks. And you?" she asked, not knowing what else to say.

"Probably not nearly as well as you, but I did just fine. I had a need to hear your sweet voice this morning, Little Darlin'," he said, being completely honest.

When she said nothing, he continued, "I just got off the phone with my brother Zane. Do you remember him?" he asked her.

"Yes, I think. He was the youngest of you three, right?"

"That's right, and I'm right smack-dab in the middle at thirty-five. Hayden is the oldest. He lives just out of town.

You'll probably see him at work tonight. He usually comes in on Fridays."

"So what did you talk about, your brother and you?"

"He's been living in California and has decided to come home. Said he'd be here in about a week. And get this, he's bringing his fiancée with him."

"Hmmm," was all she could think of to say in response, not knowing if it was a good idea to bring up marriage. After all, the man was bound and determined to drag her to the altar, and she wasn't at all sure if that was what she wanted. Better to be safe than sorry, for now at least.

"Well, Little Darlin', I need to go. I'll see you at work tonight."

"All right, Sean. I'll see you tonight," she said then hung up the phone.

Memories assailed her mind. Gossip about the wild O'Malley boys—and how they liked to share their women. With a shudder, Honor prayed that's all it was, small town gossip started by folks who had nothing better to do with their days.

She'd have to wait it out and see what happened, but she wouldn't make any decisions about staying in Texas until she knew for sure what type of man Sean O'Malley was. At this point in time though, she couldn't imagine him sharing her with anybody, not that she'd let him. After all, wasn't that why he'd punched her dance partner in the nose the other night? Because he wasn't much into sharing where she was concerned.

Chapter Four

It was Friday night, and O'Malley's was the busiest place on the block. It was an accomplishment Sean was very proud of. At a table across the room, a group of men and women were having a very boisterous conversation. Their laughter filled the place.

Absently, Sean wondered what Hayden's reaction would be when he made it in for his Friday night drink. If the energetic woman with short spiked hair was still sitting at the table laughing her head off when Hayden finally got there, it would more than likely turn into an interesting evening.

About the time he finished washing the round of dirty glasses Honor had set on the bar, she was back with more.

"Slow down, Little Darlin'," he chided her. "I can't keep up."

"I'll help then," she answered, making her way behind the bar to join him in front of the deep stainless steel double sink.

Honor had been skittish as a cat in a roomful of rockers when she had first showed up for work. It took a good thirty minutes before she would even look him in the eye, and when she finally did, she'd had the cutest look on her face.

All flustered and pink-cheeked, she looked as if she wanted the floor to open up and swallow her whole. Sean could do nothing but smile for several long minutes, which evidently rubbed her the wrong way because before he knew what was happening, she had both hands balled into fists. The way she rested them on her slender hips, foot tapping a vicious rhythm, made him well aware she was getting angry. Damn, but she was gorgeous.

Before she got going full steam ahead, he gathered her close and kissed the daylights out of her. She had no time to protest before his tongue sought refuge within the warm, moist depths of her mouth.

Her taste burst upon his tongue, wringing a groan from him. Her body was meshed with his, pliant and ready. Just as ready as he was.

The feel of his cock rubbing against her belly was sheer misery, and at the same time, overwhelmingly joyous. Holding Honor in his arms was better than jacking-off any day of the week.

Of course, the fact that they were at the pub, and it was time to open put a damper on the situation, but just that brief embrace had put her at ease and that was what he'd been going for.

He wanted her to remember every minute of every swat that had landed on her delectable backside, but coming to terms with the darker side of one's sexuality could be a tricky, emotionally draining business. So, he'd push a little here and there, just enough to keep her ultra aware, on edge, but he wouldn't ask too much of her just yet.

When Honor was standing next to him at the sink, he stared back at her in the mirror. From their vantage point, they could see the room behind them. The noisy group across the room seemed to get larger by the minute. He was grateful Honor wasn't the only one waiting tables tonight, or he'd never get the chance to be near her.

When he was sure no one was watching, he moved until he was standing directly behind her, completely blocking her from the room at large, and yet allowing her to see everyone behind them, through the mirror.

He nestled his cock against her lower back then bent his head to the curve of her neck, licking and nibbling until he reached the tender flesh of her earlobe.

Little wisps of hair smelling of strawberries tickled his nose. Bringing one arm around, he clasped her tightly to him, her back to his chest.

One hand brushed the underside of her left breast, causing a shiver to run along her body, making him smile. He let his hand continue its wicked journey. When he reached the tip of her breast, his fingers rolled and pinched the taut nipple found there. It hardened further, beading in his hand as it begged for all he had to offer.

When Honor gasped in surprise, arching her back to get closer to his hand, Sean's free hand moved under her shirt, stroking the bare skin of her abdomen.

Her skin was warm and smooth. Her flat abdomen left her ribs outlined, allowing him to trace them, causing her to squirm her ass against him. He'd have to remember she was ticklish.

The way she reacted to his touch made him feel ten-foot tall. Every little moan and gasp went straight to his cock causing it to harden as his life's blood throbbed through its veined length. The intensity made his heart feel as though it would burst from his chest, his head swam with visions of what it would be like to have Honor helpless, at his mercy.

His mind automatically swung to a vision of Honor tied to his bed, which made him wonder what she'd think of a little bondage play.

Once again, he plucked and rolled her nipples, this time one was fondled over her shirt, the other under her shirt. He could see how aroused she was. High on her cheeks, the color was a dusky pink. Her nipples were both beaded to hard peaks and her eyes, her magnificent blue eyes, were heavy with lust.

When she moved her ass against him in a silent plea for release while allowing her eyelids to close, he commanded her to open them.

"Open those baby blues, Little Darlin'. I want you to watch what I'm doing to you."

It took a moment, but her eyelids fluttered open, remaining at half-mast as if they were too heavy to open completely.

"Sean, you can't," she whispered. He loved it when she said his name in that throaty voice. Her eyes were wild as she watched the room behind her. He could feel her heartbeat against his hand, fast and strong. Was she worried someone would see them? Did the thought arouse her even more?

"Sure I can. You just relax and go with it."

He felt her stiffen just a bit when one hand inched her knee-length denim skirt up to her thighs. His fingers slipped beneath the elastic at the leg of her panties, allowing him free rein of her slick center.

Bending at the knees, Sean lowered enough to rub his engorged cock between the cleft of her ass. At the same time, he sank one finger deep inside her tight sheath, rubbing his palm against her swollen clit.

When her legs began to tremble, he held tight. Her head had lolled back against his shoulder so he reminded her once again.

Nipping her neck, he said, "Eyes open, baby."

"Oh, Sean," she panted. "Not here."

"Tell me when you're ready, Darlin'," he said, playing her body until her back bowed and her breathing came in short little bursts.

Her pussy pulled at his finger, milking it just the way her heat would milk his cock. She was extremely wet, her juices making slippery sucking noises as he worked his finger in and out of her.

The smell of her arousal as it wafted about them was enough to make him lose it. Gritting his teeth to stay in control, he continued to fuck her with his finger while working her clit with the heel of his hand.

Her mouth formed a perfect little "O" just as her eyes began to glaze over. "Oh, God, Sean…" was all she managed.

* * * * *

Honor thought she'd die from the exquisite feeling prepared to take over. She could feel her body tremble, her knees grow weak, but nothing on earth could make her say the words to stop him. Seeing the differences between them in the mirror was so erotic she could do nothing but give herself to the feelings coursing through her body.

His face, as it watched intently from over her shoulder, holding her gaze, made her dizzy with need. The tanned skin stretched taut over his high cheekbones and squared jaw was so different from the paleness of her own.

She couldn't see his hand as it played between her thighs, but the fingers torturing her nipple were insistent, causing her other nipple to tighten and press against her blouse begging for its turn.

The force of her arousal covered her body like a glove. It took every effort, every brain cell not already occupied, to stifle the scream begging to break free.

The noises her body was making as the length of his finger worked in and out of her were lewd, embarrassing, and yet, they brought her arousal to a dizzying peak. If being fondled in a crowded bar was this good, she could only imagine and anticipate what it would be like to have his penis buried deep inside her. It had been so long since she'd had a man, and never before had she had a man quite like the one standing so close behind her.

When she finally managed to say something, to warn Sean she was about to explode, the clenching of her muscles cut her off. She was so wet she could feel her liquid heat slick between her thighs. She could imagine her essence running over Sean's hand as it worked furiously within her body.

Just about the time she was no longer sure she'd be able to hold back her climaxing screams, his hand turned her face up and to the side. When Sean's coaxing lips settled over her own, she released all that she'd held in. Sean absorbed what the noisy pub didn't.

When she finally made it back to reality, she focused her gaze into the mirror studying the man behind her. A fine sheen of perspiration dotted Sean's face and his magnificently bald head. His hazel eyes now appeared to be a deep green in color, the pupils dilated.

The length of his shaft beneath his jeans was intimidating and arousing all at the same time, she could still feel it against her lower back.

Once again, he'd managed to bring her to the peak and watch her fall over without getting there himself. He was an exasperatingly confusing man.

A man she wanted to taste. She couldn't help but lick her lips, imagining how he would feel in her mouth, hot and hard.

He must have noticed the look on her face because when she turned in his arms, he held her close.

"Don't go looking at me like that, sweetheart. Not here, not now."

The words were like a cool douse of water over the head because until then she'd forgotten where she was. Still held firmly within the circle of Sean's arms, she ventured a peek over his shoulder out into the room only to be brought up short.

Sitting just on the other side of the bar was a handsome man wearing a tan Stetson.

He was a tall man with a crooked smile. His hazel eyes made her groan. Oh, God, they'd been caught. She felt like a teenager who'd been busted necking in the backseat of her boyfriend's car.

Only she hadn't been necking, she'd been brought to a screaming orgasm in the middle of a crowded bar.

Ducking her head low to cover her burning face, she told Sean that Hayden had made it.

"What's that?" he asked.

She repeated herself, but evidently he couldn't hear with her voice muffled against his chest, so he lifted her chin with a single finger and arched a brow in question.

In a whisper, she said. "Your brother is standing behind you. From the smile on his face, I'd say he's been there a while."

Sean's mouth slid into a smile of its own. Leaning down, he rubbed his lips against hers. The hair of his mustache rubbed against her mouth rasping over each and every nerve ending.

When he brought his hand up between them, inhaling deeply, she thought she'd die.

"You smell like heaven, Little Darlin', and I bet you taste like sunshine," he said, winking at her as he sucked his finger making it glisten with saliva. "Yep. Just like sunshine."

She couldn't think of a thing to say. The man was erotically outrageous and completely lacking in inhibitions.

"Now give me your mouth. Right now a kiss will have to do, but later we'll have to try out some of those naughty thoughts running around up here," he said kissing her temple before making his way to her mouth.

When he finally released her lips, she was breathless.

"I can't wait to feel your mouth on my cock," he whispered in her ear, making her gasp, before turning to his brother.

She heard them talking, but they seemed far away. How in the hell was she going to be able to work when all she could think about was going down on Sean?

Chapter Five
ℰↃ

Sean turned to face his brother. The grin covering his face was a bit wicked he was sure. It had been worth it. Every second of every little gasp had made it all worthwhile. The fact that he still hadn't found release was no problem because tonight he would remedy that.

Tonight he would sink his throbbing shaft so deep into Honor's tight little cunt she'd never forget who it was she belonged to.

The thought made him groan in frustration. He could be a patient man when necessary, but his patience was almost at an end. And from the uncomfortable fit of his jeans, due to his everlasting erection, it was none too soon.

He could tell by the look on Hayden's face he was in for it.

"Don't start, Hayden."

"Start what?" his brother answered back with a look of innocence on his face.

"You know what," Sean growled. "Just leave it," he warned. A warning Hayden evidently chose to ignore.

"So, that's the widow's niece. Sure did grow up, didn't she?"

Sean didn't bother to answer, knowing damned well he was being baited.

"To hear Zane tell it, you've gone and fallen in love. Even told the lady herself, something I hear she wasn't too pleased about."

Sean could hear the laughter in Hayden's voice and it irritated the hell out of him. He knew exactly what to say to turn the table on his big brother.

"Yep, she was about as happy being told she belonged to me as you were while Austin was spending her days chasing you around," he said, tipping his head toward the growing crowd across the bar.

The fiery little redhead across the room was sitting on the lap of the pretty boy who'd joined the crowd only moments before. And from the looks of her, she was having one hell of a good time.

Hayden's look of triumph turned into his legendary black scowl as he slid from the barstool. Just as he'd known it would, mentioning Austin had taken the heat off of him, for now.

However, he did feel a bit guilty about putting Austin on the spot. After all, she seemed to be having a good time and not hurting a soul in the process.

From the look on his brother's face though, her good times were just about over. When Hayden took his first step forward, Sean warned, "I don't want any trouble, Hayden." To which he received a grunt in response.

Austin Calhoun was a wild woman. She'd been born and raised in Texas, and insisted she'd never live elsewhere. The only daughter of a single mother, she had pretty much raised herself.

For the past month or so, she'd worked keeping books at the Big O Ranch. She teased Hayden mercilessly about the name of his ranch and enjoyed every minute of the torture she wreaked upon him.

Of course, being the proud O'Malley he was, Hayden wouldn't even think of changing the name of the ranch. It had been the Big O Ranch since the first O'Malley had tamed the land and it would remain the Big O Ranch until there wasn't an O'Malley left to run it.

He watched as Hayden strode across the room. There were always sparks when he and Austin got together. He wondered when Hayden was going to finally give up and realize those sparks could start a damned good fire if he'd fan the flame just a bit.

Hell, Austin had made no secret about the way she felt. She claimed she'd been in love with Hayden since she was nine years old.

Sean wasn't sure what had happened to change that, but something had because just recently Austin had gone from being wild to plain old hell on wheels. She'd begun taking chances and living dangerously. Not to mention her little side job. That one still pissed Hayden off whenever it was brought up.

A commotion across the room drew Sean's attention. He didn't even have to wonder what had caused such a ruckus, the raised voice said it all.

"Dammit to hell, Hayden O'Malley! You'd better put me down before I kick your cowboy ass all over Texas."

The voice got quieter and quieter the closer to the door they got, but the struggle the woman over Hayden's shoulder was putting up was pretty good considering her size.

A loud whack filled the already quiet room as Hayden slapped his palm against the denim-clad backside riding high on his shoulder. Followed by a growled, "Stay still".

"Ouch! You son of a—" was all the crowd in the bar heard before the door closed, blocking what Sean was sure would be a barrage of curse words hot enough to make the finest sailor proud.

It was going to be a hot time in the old town for those two, Sean was sure of it. He was still watching the door when Honor came to stand in front of him.

"Why didn't you stop him?" she asked, a look of outrage on her china-doll face.

"Stop him?" he repeated, not at all sure what she meant.

"Yes. Stop. Him," she enunciated as if he were slow-witted. "That was Austin Calhoun he just carried off."

"You know Austin?" he asked, not trying to hide the irritation at her attitude. Or the fact that he wasn't at all sure he wanted his future bride hanging out with Austin The Hellion.

"Yes, I know Austin. She was a few years behind me in school, but I remember her. We've met a few times since I've been back in town. So, why didn't you stop him?" she repeated.

"Because she works for Hayden, and it seems he's always saving her from one thing or another." It sounded like a good answer to him, but from the look on Honor's face, she wasn't going for it.

"Saving her? Like how? She didn't need to be saved from anything tonight."

"Maybe, maybe not," he said, then after thinking on it for a minute added. "Maybe she needed saving from herself."

* * * * *

Honor wasn't at all sure what Sean had meant by that, but from the irritated look on his face, it was no longer up for discussion.

Once again, she thought it must be a Texas thing. Or was it an O'Malley thing? It was all so confusing, but evidently, it didn't bother anyone else because not another soul in the whole room had come to her rescue. Not even the man whose lap Austin had been sitting on.

The way Hayden had strode right over to the table in his slow-rolling gait, just like the real cowboy he was, decked out in his snug-fitting Wrangler jeans and Stetson, had proven how comfortable he was with himself. He seemed confident, as if he hadn't a care in the world.

After a few words spoken in a deep voice, the pretty boy had almost upended Austin, getting her off his lap. It would have been comical if she hadn't been embarrassed on Austin's behalf.

The whole over-the-shoulder thing had been arousing, in a barbaric sort of way. Then of course, there had been the sound of Austin's bottom being smacked. That had brought a whole flood of memories to mind.

It made her center heat just thinking of what had happened between herself and Sean. She wondered if he'd thought the same thing while watching the scene unfold?

Turning, she looked back across the room. He was watching her, a knowing look on his face. His gaze brought warmth to her cheeks, which spread down across her neck and onto her chest.

Chill bumps raised her skin, only she wasn't cold. She was warm, too warm. The feel of her now-erect nipples as they rasped the lace of her bra was excruciatingly naughty. She wanted to pinch and roll them between her fingers, as Sean had done not more than an hour ago.

Tonight would be the night. She hoped with everything inside her he would follow her home or invite her over because she could no longer hold out. She had to feel his length deep within her, filling her until she was stretched so tight around him she thought she'd be split in two.

If he didn't take the initiative, she wasn't sure what she would do. Could she make the first move, insinuate herself within his grasp?

Once again, she wondered what he would taste like. Never before had she wanted to take a man in her mouth. To feel the flesh of a penis push past the barrier of her lips, hot and deep. But there was no denying it now. That was exactly what she wanted. She just had to figure how to go about getting it and what to do with it once she had it.

The whole thing was silly actually, but she'd figure it out. Pleasing Sean O'Malley after the two mind-blowing orgasms

165

he'd bestowed on her was a big deal, and she wanted nothing more than to do it right.

Later that night, after the place had been cleaned, Honor turned out the lights preparing to go home. As she did every other night, she made her way up the hall to the back room where she gathered her personal belongings.

When that was done, she retraced her steps stopping at the door to Sean's office. After knocking lightly, Honor eased the door open just a bit, but before she could say a word, Sean drew her into the room closing the door firmly behind her.

"Are the doors locked, Honor?" She could hear the want in his voice. He was wound tight, ready to explode.

"The doors?" she questioned.

"The front and back doors. Are they locked?"

"Yes, I locked them before I did the register."

"Good, very good," he said, as he lead her to the chair in front of his desk.

Honor wasn't sure what he expected of her as he removed the bag from her hand, laying it on the floor next to the desk. He then returned and sat in the chair she was standing next to.

"I can't wait, Little Darlin'. I need to feel your mouth on me now."

Honor couldn't help but lick her lips. She'd been waiting for an opening and here it was, but she was a nervous wreck. Her hands shook as she stepped closer to him.

"Right here?" she asked.

"Right here, Darlin'."

Without preamble, Honor dropped to her knees in front of him, hiking her denim skirt to mid-thigh in order to make the movement easier. He smelled so good she wanted to tear into him. Something about his manly scent turned her into a raving lunatic. Musk and spice. She wondered if he would taste as good as he smelled.

She rested her shaky hands high up on his thighs loving the way they tensed at her touch. By the look of the bulge in his pants, he'd been anticipating her visit. The thought sent a bolt of feminine awareness shooting right through her to her womb.

He wanted her, the too-tall woman with narrow hips and small breasts. It was amazing to think that for once, she didn't feel inadequate—she felt beautiful.

Looking into his handsome face, she said, "I've…um…I've never done this before."

It was hard to admit and she wasn't sure what his reaction would be, but she didn't expect the immediate look of joy she found on his face or the twinkle in his eyes when he answered.

"But you want to."

It wasn't a question so she didn't answer.

"I saw the way you looked at me earlier. Licking your lips while watching my cock almost got you in trouble," he said, as he grasped her face with both his hands.

She could feel the slight shake of his grasp. His warm palms were comforting, and yet his touch sent shivers throughout her body.

"Tell me what you want me to do, Sean. Every little detail of what you like. I want to please you."

"You already do, sweetheart. You already do."

When she tentatively reached for his zipper, purposefully brushing her hand against his rigid length, he let out a low, husky groan. The sound vibrated through his body and into hers, making the tiny hairs on her arms stand at attention.

She knew then and there that he spoke the truth. Whatever she did tonight, she knew it would please him. With that revelation, another chink in her armor had been removed.

Chapter Six
🖎

Honor's innocent fumbling would have him shooting off his load before she could get him in her heart-shaped mouth. But he wouldn't stop her — he couldn't stop her. All he would be able to do was watch as her full, sensuous lips closed around the engorged head of his throbbing cock.

Her slender hands, which were trembling slightly, pulled his T-shirt from the waistband of his jeans, her hand was warm against his flesh as she then tugged at the button. When it finally popped free, she began working on his zipper. Ever so slowly, she lowered it, rasping it down the length of his distended member. The feeling of her hands on him made him shudder.

He lifted his hips, permitting her to lower not only his jeans but also his navy-blue boxer briefs. He liked how she looked at him. Evidently his cock did too because it waved and bobbed, trying to gain her attention.

When he felt the finger of one hand trace the pulsing vein along the underside of his shaft, he couldn't help but circle her wrist with his hand, stopping her movement. She glanced up at him, her look silently questioning.

"Give me just a minute, Darlin'. Your hot little fingers are like heaven, but I'm so hot for your mouth it may be over before it starts."

Her eyes sparked, a mischievous twinkle settling in their blue depths. Once again, she licked her full and curvaceous lips until they glistened. She then walked her fingers up the inside of his thighs.

"Feel good?" she asked when he shuddered.

He couldn't say a thing, only nod his head before settling it on the chair's back.

The little vixen was a fast learner, and she evidently wanted to be in control because she gave no credence to his need for her to slow down. As a matter of fact, she seemed to be teasing him even more.

When her hot breath floated across the head of his cock, his eyes flew open, his head lifting. Looking down, all he could see was the top of her blonde head. When her moist tongue darted out the very first time, tasting him ever so quickly, he thought he'd die from pleasure.

His hands threaded their way through her hair, gathering it so he could pull it away from her face. He needed to feel her skin, to get the best view possible while she worked her mouth around his cock.

She was so velvety hot he thought he'd go up in flames. She took just the head of him in at first, flicking her tongue around and around. He had a hard time remaining in his seat.

After what seemed like hours of that torture, she settled more into her kneeling position bringing her closer to his lap, causing him to sink deeper into her waiting mouth.

One hand grasped the base of his shaft and squeezed. He couldn't help the gasp that escaped.

"Sorry," she said. "Did I hurt you?"

Oh, yeah, it hurt so good. "Nope," he said, "You're doing fine, just fine." Taking her face in his hands, he guided her mouth back to his eagerly waiting cock, sliding it between her full lips. Past the barrier of her teeth into the warm, waiting depths of her mouth. He needed for her to continue.

She looked up at him through her lashes, keeping her head slightly turned so he could see her face as she opened wide, once again taking him in.

The hand working the base of his shaft shifted until his balls were held delicately within her grasp. Her gentleness was like a balm to his overly sensitized body, calming raw nerves, yet leaving him highly aroused.

She had settled into a nice rhythm, one that would keep him floating yet not allow him to fall over too soon. The lull gave him a brief moment to study her.

Her eyes had closed—her lids wore an almost sheer tan-colored shadow. She wasn't one for a lot of make-up. He could still see the tiny blue veins winding their way just under their surface.

Her nose was small and upturned in the center of her doll-like face. Her cheeks were all roses. The way they hollowed as she sucked him in was as erotic a picture as he'd ever seen. Her lips thinned as she struggled to take more of his length. Combined, she was perfect. Absolutely perfect.

"Honor, baby," he groaned. "Take me deeper, suck me harder."

And she did.

She released his length with a plop then quickly gobbled him back up, slurping and sucking as her arousal grew. Her tongue traced the length of his shaft down until she reached his balls.

He widened his thighs as he scooted closer to the edge of the seat, giving her better access.

When her lips reached his balls, she sucked one into her mouth rolling it around with her tongue. Never had anyone done that to him. Her hand held him tightly as her thumb played with the single slit in the center of his cockhead, rubbing the fluid she found there.

The intensity waned as she released his sac only to be renewed as she worked the other side in the same way. It took every ounce of willpower he had not to come all over her hand.

She must have felt the change in him. The way his hips pumped against her hand, the sounds of carnal pleasure he could no longer hold back, because her head came up, her gaze meeting his.

Her lips were pink and puffy, and shiny with saliva. She made a movement to flick a wisp of escaped hair out of the way, but Sean still held the length tightly in his fist, allowing little movement as he leaned down to kiss her.

The kiss deepened. He plunged his tongue into her mouth over and over tasting himself. When he tried to pull her up into his lap, she shook her head backing up just a bit.

"I'm not done yet," she said in a throaty whisper. "I want to taste you, Sean."

It was her first time, and she'd done a fabulous job. It was the best blowjob he'd ever experienced, but he didn't want to give her more than she could take.

"Are you sure?" he asked, praying she'd say yes.

She nodded her head just before taking him back in her mouth. This time she was like a woman on a mission. She was to be denied nothing. Wringing every reaction his body had to offer, she then took even more.

When he felt the tingle in his spine, he knew he was close. His hands, still fisted in the silky strands of Honor's hair, sought her face, rubbing the shoulder-length locks over her smooth skin as she sucked him deep and hard.

His body tightened, his hips bucked and without another thought, he spewed his seed deep within her mouth, watching as she struggled to take all he offered.

When he was finished, she licked his flaccid cock clean then leaned back to view her work. Licking her lips, she looked up into his face and gave a triumphant smile.

Leaning in, Sean ran his finger over the corner of her mouth, catching a drop of sperm. He then put his finger to her lips and whispered, "You missed a spot, Little Darlin'," just before he kissed her.

* * * * *

The feel of Sean's penis in her mouth was wonderful. He was large, the vein running the length of him throbbing with his imminent release.

Honor felt powerful and feminine the way she was kneeling at his feet, his cock in her mouth. A part of her wondered why she'd never given head before, but her heart knew right away why — because it hadn't felt right. With Sean it felt right. Everything they did together felt right.

That first taste of pre-cum had sent her senses reeling. Something she'd always viewed as distasteful was now the very thing she craved, warm and sweet.

She could tell he was concentrating on holding off. Trying to make it last longer, but she was in charge this time, and she wanted to hear him moan with his release.

She'd been waiting for some type of instruction from him. Hoping he would walk her though it, step by step. When he made no attempt at offering up advice, she decided to just go with the flow. It seemed her instincts were working out just fine if his hip thrusting was any indication.

As she fondled his scrotum, she could feel his testicles tighten — he was getting close. When he tried to distract her with a kiss, she thought she would go crazy with the need to taste him.

After telling him she needed just that very thing, he released her, letting her have her way. He had lengthened even further. The bulbous head of his shaft was almost purple in color. No longer could she toy with him, she had to have it all. Right now.

Sinking her mouth down as far as she could, she sucked his length, hollowing her cheeks in an attempt to send him spiraling over the edge.

Her tongue played with the tip of him, flicking faster and faster as his pelvis gyrated in an attempt to gain release. She sunk lower, then rasped her way back up, sinking again all in quick strokes. One more time was all it took before his shout echoed through the room, the salty musk of his essence filling her mouth.

Working her throat, she milked him, leaving nothing behind. When his penis was soft in her mouth, she lapped at it, cleaning its length before sitting back. She could do nothing to stop the smile tilting her lips.

The feel of Sean's finger caressing her mouth brought her back to earth. When he leaned forward whispering to her, her face heated. Shame was quickly thrust aside when his finger slipped into her mouth feeding her the drop of seed he'd just rescued from the corner of her mouth. Then his lips met hers in a kiss to outdo all other kisses.

Raising herself back up onto her knees, she crawled up into his lap. Within minutes, she felt his length, once again hard, against the curve of her hip. Squirming to get closer, she whimpered. "I need to feel you inside me."

He said nothing, only moved to stand, steadying her on her feet when her wobbly knees would have buckled. Sean straightened his clothes then with a firm grasp on Honor's elbow, he tugged her toward the door.

"Let's go," was all he said.

She pulled against his grasp, receiving an irritated look in response. "Just a second, my purse," she said, when he just kept towing her out the door.

When he released her, she made quick work of retrieving her purse, not wanting to waste a second. Back at his side, she grasped his hand, threading her fingers through his. This time it was she who hauled him to the door.

She was wet and ready. Her panties felt as if they were soaked, and her empty core longed to be filled.

"Hurry, Sean, hurry," she said, panting with not only the effort to pull him toward the car, not that he was fighting, but also with her arousal.

Her flustered antics won a chuckle from the big man beside her and a shriek from herself as he upended her over his shoulder, planting a stinging slap on her bottom. Oh, yeah, it was going to be a good night, a very good night.

Chapter Seven

They couldn't get to a bed fast enough in Sean's opinion. He needed to touch and to taste. There was no denying how she stirred his blood.

After settling her into the front seat of his truck, he went around and climbed in behind the wheel. The engine rumbled to life and in a flash, they were gone.

Not normally one to speed—tonight was an exception, an emergency. If he didn't get Honor naked and into his bed real quick-like, he was going to explode.

Patting the seat, he said, "Move over here closer to me, Little Darlin'. I've got a need to touch you."

Honor scooted to the center of the bench seat and snuggled in close. Her hand wandered over his thigh causing his muscles to bunch.

"Lift this up for me, sweetheart," he said, playing with the fabric of her blue denim skirt. When her eyes shot up to his, he added, "And take off your panties. I want to see that pretty pink pussy of yours."

Her cheeks turned a beautiful shade of pink, but she did as he asked. Once she'd removed her panties and lifted her skirt to where it rested around her waist, he stroked her thigh just as she had his.

Her legs parted the tiniest bit, but it was all the invitation he needed. With one hand on the steering wheel, he played with her slick folds.

She was wet and ready and they were still a block from his place. He wasn't sure he was going to make it.

When they finally pulled up to his house, he pressed the button to open the automatic garage door. Never before had the thing seemed so slow. *I'll have to check into it*, he thought absently.

Finally, the door was opened completely so he could pull his truck into the garage, shielding them from the outside world.

When the door closed behind them, he turned toward her and pulled her into a passionate embrace. His lips devoured her, hinting at what was to come. Untucking her shirt from the waist of her skirt, he pulled it over her head, leaving her in only the two lace triangles blocking her nipples from his view. That would never do.

Honor whimpered, begging him to do more. When he didn't move fast enough, she unhooked the front clasp of her bra then tugged his head to her chest.

Sean groaned at her enthusiasm, wondering if they would ever make it to his bed. Yes, they had to. There was no way he would make love to Honor in the front seat of his pickup the first time. They'd have plenty of time for that later.

He lapped at a puckered nipple, drawing it deep into his mouth before pulling his head back, releasing it with a wet pop from his mouth.

"Enough," he growled as he opened his door pulling them through it.

Cool air hit her bared chest tightening her nipples further, causing her to look down. A confused look crossed her face before she quickly moved to cover herself from his gaze.

"No, Darlin', don't ever cover yourself from me."

She said nothing in return, but her chin shot up just a notch before she finally dropped her arms to her side.

They had finally made it to his room. It took all he had to close the door and lead her to the bed instead of taking her right there against the door.

"Lay back and let me finish getting rid of your clothes. You won't be needing them for a while."

"I want to see you, too," she said in a quiet voice.

"You will, Darlin'. You will, but not yet."

He knew if he removed all his clothes this early in the game, there wouldn't be much foreplay. He'd be inside her so quick it would make her head spin.

When she was nude before him, he allowed his eyes to feast on her. Every minute detail was stored away for a later time. Every curve, every valley was inspected and loved. He could do no less.

When she was writhing beneath him on the bed, he nipped at the lobe of her ear and whispered, "Tell me what you want, Honor."

Her body moved restlessly as he wedged a denim-clad thigh between her naked legs until it pressed firmly against her mound. She cried out as she moved to get closer.

"I want to feel you."

"Feel me where, baby? Tell me. If you want something, I want you to tell me what it is. Say all those nasty words you've never used."

"Oh, Sean, I can't," she wailed.

"You can and you will—if you want any part of this," he said, rubbing his engorged length against her thigh.

"I want…I want to feel you in me," she moaned.

"What part of me, Honor. My fingers, my tongue? Tell me," he insisted.

* * * * *

The words he was breathing against her neck, whispering in her ear were making her so hot. The way he was rubbing his thigh across her clit wasn't helping either, but saying the words was so hard.

They seemed almost foreign to her, but the naughty girl beat out the good girl this once, and before she was aware of what she was saying, the words tumbled forth.

"Lick me, Sean. I want to feel your tongue inside me."

Those words must have been the right ones because before she finished the sentence he'd thrown himself from the bed and began to undress.

His chest was massive. Corded muscle sculpted every contour of its width. His head may have been completely bald, but his chest was not. She remembered the feel of his coarse hair against her hand. Her palms itched to feel it once again.

He removed his pants leaving himself clad in only his cotton boxer briefs. They molded his hips leaving little to the imagination.

Her eyes were riveted to his groin. Nothing short of death could rip her gaze away. As he lowered the offending underwear, she noticed his strong hands. The blunt tips were clean and well maintained. His fingers were thick-looking, reminding her of how they had felt buried deep inside her cunt. What a word...cunt. It felt good to think it. To let go, and just think and say whatever came to mind. She couldn't help the shiver of anticipation coursing through her body as his briefs made the slow journey down his bulky thighs.

When his briefs were on the floor, in a puddle around his ankles, he stepped out and made his way back to the bed. When he moved to climb on the bed beside her, she held her hand out to stop him, still unable to pull her gaze from his magnificent cock.

"You're beautiful," she said. Then licking her lips, she leaned forward bestowing the head of his cock with a single kiss.

She loved the way his eyes seemed to darken—his lids drooping with lust. When he climbed onto the bed beside her, she reached out a hand in welcome.

He gently kissed the palm of her hand then trailed kisses up her arm until he'd reached her collarbone where he nipped her skin. His tongue snaked out, soothing the hurt. With quick wet flicks of his talented tongue, he worked his way down her body until he reached the downy thatch of hair covering the apex of her thighs.

"Next time I shave my head will you let me shave you here?" he asked, tugging playfully at her pubic hair, wringing a gasp from her already dry lips.

"Yes," she croaked, not sure if she liked the idea of a razor so close to her delicate place.

When his tongue stroked her engorged clit, the hair of his mustache rasping against the swollen tissues, she forgot all about her nervousness. He continued lapping at her—holding her open with the fingers of both hands, his tongue caressing each fold until she convulsed in wave after wave of release.

Without a moment's respite, he brought her back up. His mouth sought the tight little nub nestled between her nether lips. Pulling it into his mouth, he sucked relentlessly until she could handle no more.

"It's too much," she cried out at the combination of pleasure and pain.

"It's not enough," he answered as he levered himself over her.

With a hand on each thigh, he pushed her legs wide. She watched breathlessly as he guided the tip of his cock to her entrance. In one swift motion, he plunged his entire length into her.

She gasped, struggling in vain to accommodate the sheer size of him. His hips spread her legs wide, but after that single thrust, he remained still.

"Son of a bitch!" he swore. Remaining where he was he demanded, "How long has it been?"

She was on fire, the unused muscles of her vagina stretched tight around his girth. "A while," she panted. "It's been a while."

She was concentrating so intently on relaxing, she missed the look on his face. Anger and worry replaced awe.

"Why didn't you tell me, dammit?" he thundered.

What in the hell was the man raving about, and what right did he have to be mad? It was her pussy that felt as if it was being split in two.

"Are you going to yell at me or fuck me?" she demanded, her anger surfacing.

He made a choking sound at her words then began to move. At first, the stinging sensation was too much, but before she had the chance to protest, the burn of pain turned into a mind-numbing burn of pleasure and she found herself moving with him. Meeting him stroke for stroke. Thrust for thrust.

"Like this, Little Darlin'?" he asked. "Is this how you want me to fuck you?"

"Yes, yes," she screamed as the walls of her pussy tightened around his shaft, keeping him buried deep within her depths until she felt the warm splash of his cum as it jetted from him into her.

The man was amazing. Not only had he turned her into a wanton creature who was willing to do naughty things in public, but now she was cursing on top of it. And she'd started with the worst word of all, but boy-oh-boy did it ever feel good.

When her body finally settled down, with no more aftershocks clenching her vaginal muscles, he pulled ever so slowly from her.

Rolling onto his side, he took her along with him. "You should have told me." The words were an accusation deflating the cloud she'd been riding high on.

"It's okay, Sean. You didn't hurt me."

Her words seemed to soothe him. Nothing more was said. Honor was drifting off to sleep when Sean's chest began to shake. A deep rumble followed.

It took her a minute to realize he was laughing. His laugh was infectious. Without even knowing the reason, she joined him. In moments, the stress of losing her aunt and finding herself alone in Texas, thrust into a relationship she wasn't sure she wanted had melted, to be replaced with emotions she wasn't sure she was ready to deal with.

"What's so funny?" she asked when she'd calmed down enough to catch her breath.

"You, sweetheart. Not a bad word in sight and then you go and drop a bomb like the F-word." He began to laugh again.

"Well," she said, punching him in the ribs. "You said you wanted me to talk dirty. Besides, you made me mad yelling at me like that."

It seemed like a perfectly good reason to Honor, but the words sobered Sean instantly.

"If you ever pull a stunt like that again, I'll put you over my knee. I won't allow you to do anything that might hurt you." When he seemed to get a hold of his temper once again he muttered, "All you had to do was speak up, and I'd have slowed down." Of course, he wasn't a hundred percent sure that was the honest truth, but that was his story and he was sticking to it.

"Promises, promises," she taunted, thinking another spanking might not be such a bad thing.

Heck, this bad-girl stuff wasn't as hard as she thought it would be. Wasn't there some saying that a man might want a lady in public, but it was a whore he wanted in the bedroom? From this day forth that would be her new goal, to be the best of both worlds.

The thought brought a smile to her lips. Her eyes began to droop. The last thought that filtered through her mind before she drifted off to sleep was that soon she would have a pussy just as bald as Sean's head.

Chapter Eight
ꕥ

The next morning dawned way before Sean was ready for it. Squinting his eyes against the sun filtering through the gaping curtains, he climbed out of bed. The first order of business was a steaming cup of coffee.

Scratching his chest, he headed to the kitchen, but before leaving his room, was instead sidetracked by a noise.

Humming. It took a second for his mind to clear, and the previous night to work its way past his bleary-eyed morning confusion.

His cock immediately sprang to life at the vivid memories. Honor's fist-tight pussy gripping every hard inch of him. The scent of her juices as they overflowed onto his questing fingers.

Without a second thought to invading her privacy, he made his way to the bathroom. Standing in the doorway, he could see her silhouette through the haze of steam filling the air.

She has the voice of an angel, he thought to himself, wondering if she'd ever considered singing in public. The haunting melody he'd first heard her humming had turned into a rollicking version of *You Don't Mess Around With Jim*.

As she belted out the verse about Big Jim being a pool shootin' son of a gun, Sean grabbed a bath towel from the cabinet. By the time she made it to the chorus, he was hard and ready, making his way to the shower.

Her back was turned to him, showing off the curve of her ass to perfection. The valley of her spine was erotic as hell. He couldn't wait to trail his tongue down it, nipping and tasting every square inch. Opening the glass shower door, he stepped in and took Honor into his arms.

"Oh!" she shrieked. "You scared me to death," she added, when she'd finally found her voice.

"I didn't want to interrupt your song, Darlin', but I couldn't stay away once I saw you in here all naked and wet. Nice song, by the way," he added with a wink.

"Thanks," she relied saucily. "It reminded me of you."

"How's that?"

"Well, you shoot pool like a pro, just like Jim. And you're big, really big," she said, looking down to the juncture of his thighs where his cock was standing proudly erect, begging for attention.

"But you're not dumb and they don't call you boss," she finished with a giggle.

"Why thank you, sweetheart. I think the 'boss' title is saved for Hayden. As for the rest, what can I say? I own a bar so I'd better know how to shoot pool, and I've always been big." He let loose his best roguish smile and gave a quick wink before backing her to the shower wall.

With a hand flat against the tiled wall on each side of Honor's head, he trapped her. She looked from side to side as if looking for an escape route before leaning into him, nipping his lower lip.

The sensation was magnetic. It drew him to her swiftly and without thought. When he leaned closer, she grasped his cock in one delicate hand and gave a tiny squeeze. Letting go, she then fondled his balls, causing his shaft to grow impossibly longer and harder.

Tugging firmly but gently, she forced him to move until they were out of the direct spray of water before she gracefully dropped to her knees in front of him.

There was no play in her game this time. She zeroed in on him then lowered her head devouring him in one swift motion.

It was almost enough to send him over the edge. In order to remain standing, he locked his knees and leaned against the cool tiled wall of the shower.

The woman was a fast learner — he'd give her that. Lord, but she could win a prize with what that delectable little mouth could accomplish. Good thing she belonged to him because if he ever heard of her mouth settling on another cock, there would be hell to pay.

That was his last coherent thought before she hummed while keeping his length buried damned near to the back of her throat.

The ensuing vibration was like setting a match to kindling. It caused him to go up in flames. And once again, she took everything he had to offer.

* * * * *

He said she tasted like sunshine. Well, if that was the case then she would have to say he tasted like a starry moonlit night.

Dark and mysterious.

From the moment he'd stepped foot into the shower, without batting an eye at either her nudity or his own, Honor had been lost.

One glimpse of his beautifully nude body, especially his proudly erect penis, and her mouth had watered for a taste. There was no fighting the urge to take him in her mouth, to love him, to honor the man that he was. When he'd trapped her against the shower wall, he'd given her the perfect opportunity to do just that.

Now she watched as he soaped up one of those fluffy shower puffs. It was an incredible sight. To see this overly large man lather up a cute baby blue shower puff. When he moved toward her and began to run the puff along her neck and chest, she couldn't move a muscle.

185

After washing them both thoroughly, he stepped from the shower and gathered two bath towels. Honor stood on the fluffy bathmat while Sean dried her from head to toe, paying extra special attention to the strategic spots he knew would make her body tingle and her mind whirl in anticipation.

Honor watched as he dried his body then wrapped the towel around his waist. He opened a drawer, pulling several items from it. It was his shaving equipment.

"Come here, Little Darlin'," he said.

Without question, she moved to his side. Honor watched as he lowered the toilet lid and sat down.

"How about you shave me then I'll shave you?" he asked.

"Ummm," she answered, trying to think of an excuse when he cut her off.

"Uh-uh, last night you said 'yes' when I brought it up."

"That's not fair. Last night I probably would have agreed to anything."

"Awww, come on, Darlin'. You'll love it, I promise."

"Why do you shave your head, Sean?" It was something she'd often wondered about.

"No special reason at first, but now I can tell you that when rubbed just the right way it makes me horny as hell."

She laughed for a minute, studying him she said, "If I touch your head..." She couldn't finish, it seemed preposterous.

"If you don't believe me just wait until that pretty little cunt of yours is bald. Then you'll understand. It's so much more sensitive, especially when freshly shaved."

Hearing him refer to her vagina as a cunt was extremely provocative. It seemed strange considering the fact that if it had come from someone else, she would have taken it as an insult. With Sean though, it made her hot and wet.

After thinking about it, she agreed. *What did she have to lose besides a bit of pubic hair?* She mentally shrugged.

Following Sean's directions, she first used his electric razor.

That alone made his head feel smooth to the touch, but he insisted she lather him up and use a regular razor as well. Stroking her hand over the denuded skin of his scalp, she wondered if her shaving his head had any effect on him.

Leaning forward, she looked over his shoulder to ask him when she noticed how the towel over his groin was tented. Question answered. She couldn't help the bright smile curving her mouth.

For the first time in her life, she felt at home. To be content knowing she would be staying in one place was new to her. Her heart screamed for her to tell Sean, but she couldn't bring herself to do it. The man had an ego the size of Texas, and she wasn't about to inflate it any further by telling him he was right.

Lord have mercy, he'd really be impossible to live with then!

Once finished, she wiped any excess foam from his head then patted him dry with a towel. Peeking over his shoulder to his lap, she whispered, "I believe you." After nipping his neck, she turned and sauntered from the room.

She could hear his laughter as he followed her from the bathroom. When she turned, it was to see him place a can of shave foam and a new razor on the nightstand beside the bed.

"Lay down on your back with the towel under your hips, sweetheart. I'll be right back."

He walked from the room back into the adjoining bathroom. Minutes later he emerged with a bowl full of what looked like steaming water and a pair of scissors.

Honor did as he asked. She climbed onto the bed and got into the position he specified with her towel under her hips, leaving her whole body naked before him. He didn't seem to mind in the least.

He came to the edge of the bed and took her calves in his hands, pushing back until her feet were flat on the bed, knees wide, leaving her completely open.

She could feel the heat spread all the way to the roots of her hair as he continued to gaze at her vagina, which was sure to be wet.

He began by clipping the hair as short as possible with the scissors. Honor hummed to herself trying to keep at least a small amount of dignity. Staying as he'd placed her was not an easy task when what she really wanted to do was close her legs, grab her towel and cover herself.

Once he'd clipped her pubic hair short, Sean covered her mound with shaving cream. The feel of his fingers spreading the think cream over her partially denuded skin wasn't much help in relaxing her, not once he lifted the razor from the nightstand. When her body stiffened in anticipation, there was nothing she could do to relax it.

"Relax and enjoy, baby," he soothed, as he began to make sure strokes with the razor, removing a section of hair each time.

As each section of hair was removed, she anticipated the worst, only to find a pleasant tingling sensation instead. The cool air of the room made her even more aware of just how much coverage her pubic hair had afforded her.

What seemed like hours later, Honor was standing before a mirror with Sean right behind her. It was the first time she could ever remember seeing herself bare. Not even as a young girl had she looked at herself so closely.

When Sean moved in front of her and dropped to his knees, blowing a warm breath across her freshly shaven flesh, she came on the spot. Her cry of surprise filled the room, but didn't slow him down. With relentless determination, he showed her just how sensitive her bald mound could be. By the time he was done with her, she was a boneless heap on the floor.

He scooped her up into his arms and made off with her to the bed. It seemed the man was forever carrying her off somewhere.

Chapter Nine

ဢ

The next week seemed to pass by in a blur of activity. Every morning found Sean waking with a peaceful feeling of contentment surrounding him, Honor in his arms. Each night he took her to his home, making her more and more his.

The thought of her leaving him, leaving Texas, was enough to mess up even the best wet dream. She was his now just as much as he was hers, and the sooner she got that through her thick head, the better off they'd be.

The only problem was that everything was not okay. Oh, sure, she may be acting like her naturally happy self, but something was bothering her, and as long as she wasn't willing to tell him what it was, he couldn't help her.

That left a very frustrated Sean, which wasn't a good thing.

Besides Honor and the sheer joy he felt every time she was near, Sean had another reason to be ecstatically happy. His baby brother had made it home.

Zane seemed happy with the woman he had brought with him. Serena seemed to be the other half of Zane, and as much as Sean didn't want to admit it, he was a bit jealous.

Sean had loved many women over the years. He'd loved some for their bodies and some for their intelligence while others he'd loved for their sense of humor.

Out of all of those women, he had never loved the complete package. With Honor, it was different. He genuinely loved everything about her. He was learning, though, that while loving came easy to him, being in love did not.

It was hard work. Work he was more than willing to put in overtime for, he just hoped that Honor felt the same.

All of the uncertainty, combined with the fact he was sure something was bothering her, left him in a foul mood.

He just couldn't shake the feeling that something was going to happen to mess up what he and Honor had going. Pushing the fear aside, he decided not to give it another thought. Why go looking for trouble?

About the time he decided to leave off the bad thoughts and do whatever necessary to get himself in a better mood, the door to the pub opened.

The place was eerily quiet. The only noise was coming from the jukebox. A soft country ballad. The lights were dim, leaving the room in an amber glow.

When she walked through the door, his heart skipped a beat. The light from outside shone so brightly he could not see her face, only sunshine radiating from around her head and body like a halo, her golden aura.

She advanced into the room allowing the door to close behind her. He'd seen it before. Noticed it in every nuance of her body. The way she carried herself, the pallor of her skin. She spent her days trying to keep her distance and for the life of him, he couldn't figure out what was wrong or why she was doing it.

Every night she came alive in his arms. He'd done things to her and with her that no other woman had condoned. He'd given her her first taste of bondage, letting him tie her to his four-poster bed like a virgin sacrifice. Memories of the things they'd done while she was tied and at his mercy drained all the blood from his brain.

Like any hot-blooded male, the blood flowed directly south of his belt buckle, and pooled in his cock, which was now throbbing to life.

Although he was one hundred and ten percent sure she enjoyed every second of their time together, it seemed lately that there was a dark storm cloud gathering high above just waiting to dump its dreary load on their unsuspecting heads.

Sean studied her face as she came closer. The pain in her eyes was hard to look at. It was blatantly obvious to all that she was suffering. Or at least it was to him.

Not being able to help was like a knife being twisted in an already ragged wound. His worst fear was that she had realized she didn't love him, and she couldn't figure out how to tell him. Did she want to leave him already? And if so, would she also be leaving town?

Her chin was angled stubbornly, warning that she was going to try yet again to remain aloof. It made Sean beyond angry that she would even try after he'd spent every possible free moment loving her thoroughly.

When she reached the bar where he was standing, she rested her forehead against his chest for a brief moment surprising him. Taking a deep breath, she lifted her face offering her mouth to him.

Eagerly, he claimed her lips in a passionate kiss. Pouring every bit of himself into her, he silently prayed that everything would turn out just fine.

When he finally ended the kiss, he was breathing hard. The weight of his rigid shaft an uncomfortable reminder of the amount of control he was lacking when it came to Honor Rollings.

With his finger, he tipped her head back until he was staring down into her eyes. Eyes that were red-rimmed as if she had been crying. Eyes that suddenly seemed haunted and were no longer dancing with merriment. Blue eyes with bruises of fatigue smudged below them.

Not only did she look exhausted, but she acted as if the weight of the world was on her shoulders. And yet, when he asked, she denied anything was wrong.

With one last maddening kiss, he held her at arm's length. No longer would he stand for her evasive answers. She would tell him what was wrong right now or he would call the doctor.

She needed sleep and she needed to share her burdens, and if she wouldn't see to it herself, he sure as hell would.

* * * * *

"Hey there, handsome," she said after the last quick kiss. He was holding her away from him when all she wanted to do was burrow deep inside him and not come back out until it was all over.

"Hey, yourself," he answered. He had a very determined look on his face and the dark scowl crossing his features didn't bode well for somebody, Honor just hoped it wasn't for her. She wasn't at all sure she could take an argument right now.

"We need to talk, sweetheart," he told her while leading her to a stool. With his hands at her waist, he boosted her up onto the high barstool.

When she was comfortably seated, he wedged her knees open with a palm on each leg. Settling himself between her open legs, he blocked any chance she had of shifting away from him. This made her nervous.

"What's up?" she asked with what she hoped to be a smile on her face.

"I don't know, Honor. Why don't you tell me?"

He was angry, but she wasn't sure why. He'd asked her several times over the past few days what was wrong. She wanted to tell him, to share with him what she lived through yearly, but couldn't bring herself to do it.

Talking about the death of her parents, even all these years later, was hard. Reliving their deaths—the accident—it was all too much. There were so many good memories she longed to share but right now, so close to the anniversary of their death and the loss of her last living relative, not even the good memories were easy.

With an overly bright smile plastered on her face she said, "I don't know what you're talking about. I came in a little early so I could see you." Then to distract him, "Aren't you happy to see me?"

"Don't give me that crap, baby. You're here early because you more than likely couldn't sleep. You haven't slept well in days, tossing and turning through the night. I want to know why, Honor."

When she opened her mouth to protest, he cut her off.

"Don't even think to argue with me. You look like hell. Either you tell me what's going on or I call Dr. Thompson. Your choice."

He was right and she knew it, but it still made her spitting mad that he would insist she see a doctor.

Nightmares had kept her awake the past few nights. It was disturbing to know in her heart that nothing she might have done could have changed the outcome of her parent's accident and yet, the 'what ifs' had the ability to drive her crazy. The one big difference was that now she wasn't in it alone. Now she'd wake in a cold sweat within the circle of Sean's arms as he cooed words of comfort to her.

The dream was always the same. It was her sixteenth birthday and she was all dressed up. The Major and her mother were due any minute. She was a young woman now and would be treated as such. As a gift, her parents had bought her a new car.

They had taken a cab to the dealership to pick the car up. Her mom had made dinner reservations at a fancy French restaurant, they were going to surprise her with the car and then let her drive them to dinner. Only they never made it.

When the doorbell rang it had been a uniformed police officer. At first, she hadn't believed him. How could her parents have been killed in a car accident when their car was parked in the garage?

"There must be some mistake, officer," she'd cried, hysteria already setting in, but she knew—it was late and The Major was never late.

"I'm sorry, dear," he'd said, as he patted her trembling hand.

It was then that she learned the car her parents had been driving was for her. It was to have been a gift. A gift that had ultimately killed the two people she had loved most in the world.

If that hadn't been bad enough, the next day would forever register in her mind. She was the only living blood relative in the vicinity so it was up to her to identify the bodies of her mother and her father.

Never again would she be able to remember her mother as the mild-mannered beautiful woman that she had been, a lady through and through. Forever in her mind The Major would be a bruised and battered body, not the strong and commanding, yet loving man she'd known all her life. These were the nightmares that kept her awake night after night so close to the anniversary of their death.

After that fateful day, her life had changed. Not only had she lost her parents, but in a matter of days, she would also lose her home. They had lived on base—there was no choice but to leave. Moving often had been hard, but this time around, she'd managed to make several friends. They would also be lost to her.

It was a lesson she never forgot, and a reason why she did everything possible to not get too close to people or let others get too close to her. Somehow, Sean had found a way around the walls she so carefully erected and straight into her heart.

She'd talked herself into just having an affair. That she could handle, or so she'd thought. But as one day blended into another, Honor began to realize just how deeply involved she was.

How could she explain it to him? Would he understand her need to keep her heart safe and sound? Honor didn't think so. God, how had she gotten herself in this mess? To go from a simple fling to falling in love was the worst possible thing that could happen right now.

Honor knew Sean wouldn't understand. He wanted her for his own and he wasn't one to back down from a challenge. He would fight her tooth and nail. For that reason alone, she couldn't tell him.

"Nothing is wrong, Sean, and I don't need a doctor. What I need is for you to stop hounding me! I'm just feeling a bit under the weather. Maybe I should take a day or two off until I feel better."

"I agree. I think you do need some time off, but I won't stop hounding you," he all but sneered the words.

"I love you, dammit, and I won't stand by and watch while you make yourself sick. You've got two days, Honor. If I don't see some improvement within that time, I'll personally take you in to see Doc Thompson, kicking and screaming the whole way if necessary. Now get your ass home and get in bed before I change my mind."

"Fine!" Honor yelled at him needing to vent some of her anger. She then turned back the way she'd come and left the pub. *The man was a monster*, she thought, right before she burst into tears.

Chapter Ten

ဢ

If she didn't answer the phone, he was going to break her door down. Two days felt like an eternity. When he'd first sent her home, not only had he worried, but he'd been pissed as hell.

He had wanted to her to go to his home, but instead she went back to her tiny hole-in-the-wall apartment and had since refused to come out.

When she didn't answer the door at first, he had left thinking she was probably sleeping but as the day grew late he began to worry.

Then when she didn't answer the phone or the door, he felt sick. Deciding to try one more time before calling in the police, he dialed her number. On the fourth ring, she finally answered.

"Hello," the voice on the other end of the phone answered wearily.

"Honor? Honor, baby, is that you?" he asked.

"Hi, Sean. What did you need?" Her voice had gone from weary to angry in a second flat.

"I need to know why you aren't answering your damned door. Tell me that. And while you're at it, why aren't you answering your phone?" He knew damned well he'd get nowhere by venting his anger, but he was mad and worried.

He wanted to throttle her or better yet, put her over his knee and paddle her ass for worrying him. That idea brought a whole new meaning to being frustrated.

"You told me to go home and rest. That is exactly what I'm trying to do. I was going to call you in just a bit anyway. I know my two days are almost up," she said a bit testily. "I'm feeling a lot better so I'll be in to work tonight."

Well hell, she'd just blown the wind from his sails. He wanted to rant and rave like the maniac he felt like, but the thought of seeing Honor put everything into perspective.

He didn't care why, he just knew he had to see her. To hold and touch her.

"Okay, Little Darlin'. If you think you're up to it."

"I am, Sean. I'll see you in a while."

He wanted to shout it to whoever would listen. Honor was coming back—she would be fine. God, how he had worried.

She still wasn't in the clear. She had made him worry by not answering her door or the phone, and for that she would pay and pay dearly.

Running through his mind was all the different ways he would make her pay. She would enjoy every single moment of it so it wasn't actually punishment, but he wanted her to remember whom she belonged to.

He wanted every muscle in her lithe body to ache pleasantly from the workout he was planning to give it. He could picture the many positions he would take her in. Teasing her until she confessed what was wrong sounded promising. And from the ever-growing bulge in his pants, his cock agreed.

The past two days had crawled by at a snail's pace. Not having Honor by his side made him feel as though he was missing a piece of his heart.

Sleep was hard to come by, and when he was finally able to drift off, it was only to toss and turn and worry. Hours upon hours had been spent thinking the worst while praying for his dreams to come true.

And all the while he couldn't get visions of her out of his head. The things they had done together. Things she had done to him and how much he enjoyed returning the favor.

Just thinking about her taste, her smell, left him breathless. Sunshine and feminine musk, there was nothing better.

In the back of his mind, he could hear the small mewling noises she made while he was pleasuring her and seeking his own.

It was easy to remember how she'd thrash on the bed as he lapped ever so slowly at the petals of her sex. With her knees bent and open wide, he could feast like a hungry man introduced to a buffet table for the first time.

The fact that she was always eager take him in her mouth and taste him made every experience like heaven and hell all rolled in one.

His body would react instantly. It would take everything he had to hold his release, she was that good. The feel of her warm mouth covering his rigid cock was torture in its own way and he loved every minute of it.

So, she would be coming to work today. Well, he'd be making damned sure she went home with him after work. He wouldn't take no for an answer. This time he'd have his way in the matter. She needed someone to watch out for her until she could work her way through whatever it was bothering her and he planned to be the one to do it.

He'd let it go on long enough. Her stubborn refusal to admit her feelings even though he could see the depth of them every time he looked in her eyes worried him. The way she'd started distancing herself made him angry. Sean figured it was about time to do something about her newly found stubborn streak, at least when it concerned their relationship.

If she would just confide in him, it would make things so much easier, but she was as stubborn as they come. He wasn't much better so it seemed they would forever clash in that aspect, but that was something he could deal with.

Tonight she would tell him what was wrong. He would do his damnedest to listen and stay calm, but if she thought to leave him then she had another think coming, because that wasn't something he could or would allow to happen.

And if she didn't cooperate, he would put her over his lap once again until she finally agreed. His cock twitched in remembrance, his palm itched. He was ready.

* * * * *

Why would this year be so much worse? Honor wondered as she dressed. It didn't make any sense, but the dreams just wouldn't leave her alone. Why couldn't she just remember the good times she'd spent with her parents and let the tragedy of their death go?

Because they hadn't killed their parents.

The thought came as a flash of pain to an already exhausted mind. It had taken a sixteen-year-old Honor a couple of years before she realized she hadn't killed her parents. The love and patience of her aunt had been a big help. So why then, every single year, did the niggling pain of self-blame make her life hell?

Normally she was able to ignore everything until the day of the anniversary. Then she'd let it all out, suffer the day or two after and go on as before. It seemed that wasn't at all how it was going to happen this year. This year, with the death of her aunt, her last living relative, she was doomed to a week of hell and Sean wasn't making it any easier.

Over the past two days, the realization had set in. She was in love. If being in love was supposed to be such a wonderful thing, then why did it hurt so badly?

Honor wanted nothing more than to tell Sean of her love and never leave Texas or his arms again, but it couldn't happen. The thought of giving her heart to another, only to lose them, made her chest ache. As long as she didn't say the words out loud, she could deal with it. She'd learn to deal with the sickening fear because the only other alternative would bring as much, if not more, pain.

The thought of leaving left her feeling bereft and alone.

The ache in her head was a reminder of what the day would be like. Sean wouldn't make it easy for her. He was bound and determined to find out what was wrong, and in doing so would hurt them both.

Maybe it would be better if she just came clean, told him everything and hoped for the best. While brushing her hair, she gave it further thought, deciding against the idea almost immediately. If she admitted her feelings, there would be no turning back. Not with a man as possessive as Sean O'Malley.

Drinking herself into oblivion last night probably hadn't been the best idea she'd ever had, but it helped her to sleep, and that was exactly what she'd needed.

Today her head was suffering slightly as a result, but the dark circles under her eyes weren't nearly as pronounced.

Several hours later, she was once again making her way to the door of O'Malley's Pub. Taking a few deep breaths, she opened the door and went inside. It was going to be a long night.

It took a minute for her eyes to adjust to the dimly lit interior. Making her way across the room, she noticed there were already people seated at the bar.

Sean had a gorgeous smile on his face as he talked to the man and woman seated across from him. A bit uncomfortable with the thought of intruding, Honor made her way to the bar politely nodding to the couple Sean was speaking to.

"Hi, Little Darlin'," Sean said, snagging her by the waist, bringing her close for a long searing kiss.

Her cheeks heated in embarrassment at being kissed so intimately in front of others.

"Sean," she gasped when he finally released her.

"Someone's here to meet you, sweetheart." His head tilted toward the couple watching them. "Honor, I'd like you to meet my brother Zane. And this is his fiancée Serena."

Honor could feel her cheeks heat even more. She was probably flushed to her roots. Darn the man! First he fondles her in a crowded bar getting caught by Hayden and now he kisses her breathless in front of Zane. What they must think of her?

With as much calm as she could manage, she held out her hand, first to one and then the other. "Nice to meet you both."

Yep, it was going to be a very long night.

"Sean's been telling us all about you," Zane said to her with a twinkle in his eye, making Honor wonder exactly what all Sean had shared. Her thoughts were interrupted when Zane added, "I'm sorry for your loss. I remember your aunt. She was a wonderful person."

"Thank you," she choked out, pain slamming into her. She tried to hide her pain. To cover the way his words had affected her, but she was afraid she hadn't done too good of a job by the way the three were looking at her.

Clearing her throat, she said, "Well it was very nice meeting you. I need to get ready for my shift. I'll be back in just a minute."

She could feel Sean's eyes burning into her back as she walked down the hall and into the back room. Afraid he would follow, Honor hurriedly put away her bag. After tying her apron around her waist, she made her way back into the main room of the establishment.

Zane and Serena still sat at the bar, Sean standing behind it. Honor could tell just by the way his eyes followed her around the room that he was concerned. He was also angry, and that left her a bit concerned herself. Sean was not the type of man you wanted angry with you. He may seem like a big teddy bear with his burly physique and ready smile, but he could be closer to a grizzly when crossed.

Once again, it seemed to Honor that she had spent most of the night avoiding Sean. She was a bit sad to see Zane and

Serena go. She wanted to get to know them, but now was not the right time.

Not one to drink, it bothered Honor that alcohol was the only way she could figure out to deal with the overwhelming pain.

Sean would probably spank her again if he knew she'd been sneaking drinks throughout her shift. Her mind buzzed with the thought. It probably wouldn't be such a bad thing, a spanking. She couldn't help the giggle that escaped her lips. It was followed by a hiccup.

Maybe she'd had just a bit too much to drink tonight. She should have waited until she got home, but it had been a long shift. When the place finally cleared out, Honor made her way to the storeroom to collect her things.

On tiptoes, she made her way back up the hall in hopes of escaping before Sean caught up with her. She breathed a sigh of relief when she made her way back into the main room.

Fumbling through her purse, Honor searched for her keys. Darned fingers just wouldn't cooperate. When she finally found them in her bottomless pit of a bag, she started her way to the door.

The room tipped and swayed causing her to drop her keys. In the back of her mind, she knew it was a very stupid idea to drive, but if she called for a cab, she would have to wait. Asking Sean was out of the question because then he would know she was three sheets to the wind. Then all hell would break loose.

Another giggle escaped as she bent over to pick up her keys. She stumbled and fell but before she hit the floor, a very large arm banded around her waist hauling her back up.

"Where are you off to in such a hurry?" a deceptively calm voice asked from behind her.

"Home."

"And just how were you planning on getting there?"

"Uhhh, well—" The arm around her tightened, almost painfully, causing the air to whoosh from her lungs, leaving her unable to speak.

"Don't even think about lying to me, baby. Do you think I didn't notice you hitting the bottle all night? And now you plan on driving home. I ought to—"

This time his words were the ones cut off. "You ought to what?" she asked belligerently. "You have no say in it, Sean. Now let me go."

To punctuate the force of her words, she kicked her legs in a struggle for release.

Chapter Eleven

ഓ

If it wasn't so disturbing, it would have been comical, Sean thought to himself. He hadn't known Honor for long, but he did know enough to realize that she wasn't a drinker.

So, the fact that she had spent half of the night sneaking swigs and the other half avoiding him royally pissed him off.

With his arms full of thrashing woman, he made his way to the pool table. When he could no longer hold her wriggling body safely, he plopped her down on the green felt of the table, keeping a firm grasp on both her thighs when she tried to get down.

"Sit still, dammit!" he growled. All her wiggling around was turning his fury into arousal, and he didn't want to be aroused right now. Right now, he wanted answers.

"What in the hell is wrong with you, woman?"

"Don't 'woman' me, Sean O'Malley. And let me up. I don't have to sit here and take this from you." Once again, he held tightly as she tried to get off the pool table.

When she didn't cease her struggling, he stepped closer, insinuating himself between thighs she tried to keep closed.

His superior strength won out. Without much effort, he pried her knees apart and took another step until he was nestled into the valley he'd created. *So much for not getting aroused*, he groaned inwardly.

"You do have to sit there, and you will until I let you up. Now tell me what in the hell is going on," he demanded of her.

The look of panic and pain on her pale face made him hurt. Why was she being so damned stubborn?

"You'll tell me, Honor. Before I let you out of this place, you'll tell me everything I want to know."

He saw the change take over her face. Her eyes went from wide and panicked to hooded and sensual. She was still unstable, acting as if the room were spinning, which in her head, it probably was.

He felt a bit of guilt at the thought of taking advantage of an inebriated woman, but it only lasted a minute. In the next instant, Honor had her body wrapped around his as tight as a clinging vine. Her warm breath washed over him. She had been chewing gum, probably to throw him off. He couldn't help but chuckle at the thought.

Her tongue boldly sought the depths of his mouth, tracing the underside of his top teeth before thrusting deep. The groan rumbling from deep within his chest was purely animal in nature.

Instinct took over, leaving no room for thought, and before he knew what was happening, he had Honor sprawled out on the pool table.

It seemed hours before he finally had her out of her clothes. Her fumbling fingers had been no help at all. Legs spread wide, he pulled her close until her wonderfully wet mound was perched right at the edge of the table.

For a moment, he did nothing more than watch. Her breathing was rapid, the blatant evidence of her arousal glistening off the smoothly shaven skin of her sex.

So, she's kept herself shaved? It thrilled Sean to no end, but from now on, he wanted to do the shaving himself.

"Sean," she said barely over a whisper.

His face was close to her pussy, smelling deeply of her musk as he answered. "What, Honor?" he said, while blowing over her slightly distended clit.

"You're killing me," she groaned. "Would you do something already?"

With two fingers, he circled her folds. "Like what, baby?"

She was squirming around, trying to get closer to his face. He obliged with one long swipe of his tongue causing her to gasp and shudder. "Tell me, Honor. What is it you want me to do?"

"I want to feel your tongue in me, Sean. Then I want you to fuck me, hard and fast."

He was still unused to her speaking in such terms, even though he'd insisted on it, but damn if it didn't make his cock stand up and take notice. From the strained sounds of her breathing, he figured she was feeling the same way.

"My pleasure, Little Darlin'. My pleasure."

He couldn't hold himself back any longer. Plunging his tongue deep, he tasted of her. Sipped and slurped every drop of juice her body had to give.

Her moans and purrs of pleasure set him on fire. When the muscles of her entrance clasped around his tongue in tiny spasms, he knew she was getting close.

He sucked her, one swollen nether lip then the other, all the while paying homage to her clit with the pad of his finger.

Rubbing round and round, until her hips bucked and she wailed her frustration. When she was at the end of her rope, he circled her tiny bundle of nerves with his tongue before latching onto it with both lips, drawing it deep.

He thrust two fingers into her tight sheath, sucking her engorged flesh until she screamed with her release. Even as her body was recovering, he found it very hard to give up his spot between her legs. But the throbbing length of his shaft was making demands of its own.

* * * * *

Her head might be spinning and feel as if it were in a cloud, but her body had no such problem. Every nerve ending tingled in anticipation. Every inch of flesh felt as though it was on fire with the want and need her body felt.

The things this man could do to her. The things he made her feel. It was too much.

"No more, Sean. No more. Please, I can't take anymore."

"Yes, you can and you will. You started this, Honor, but I'm going to finish it here and now. Then tomorrow we'll talk."

It was a promise. She heard it in his voice. A part of her was beyond excited at the thought of him taking her right there on the pool table. The part that bothered her was the fact that he wanted to know her deepest, darkest secrets. In fact, he insisted on it.

"Up and at 'em, Little Darlin'."

He pulled her to a sitting position making her head swim. Before she could protest the sudden move, she was lowered from the table to stand on her own two feet, and then turned.

Looking over her shoulder, she tried to see what Sean was doing.

"Uh-uh, you stay just where I put you." His voice was low and gruff making chill bumps appear on her skin.

"Sean—" she began only to be cut off.

"Quiet."

When he moved up behind her, tapping the inside of each of her feet, forcing her to spread them wide, she grew weak in the knees. His hand sought her overly sensitive flesh.

Moving over the back of her neck, his lips nibbling as he leaned into her giving her no choice but to bend at the waist over the pool table. The position left her open and vulnerable to his every desire.

Not that she wanted to get away, but a little struggle and a little fight made it so much more fun.

Trying to turn, she once again called his name. When the loud whack sounded, followed by a burning sting on the curve of her bottom, both surprise and exhilaration flowed through her body.

"I told you to be quiet and to stay still."

"Oh, God, more, Sean. More," she groaned, giving him permission to do with her as he pleased.

The smattering of swats to follow landed in a steady barrage leaving her time to do little but gasp at the intensity of the pleasure and pain she felt. The pain fled quickly leaving her with insurmountable pleasure, too much for one woman to handle.

When she was just about to beg for her release, she heard the rasp of his zipper. The thick head of his penis nudging its way into her overflowing sex soon followed.

In one quick thrust, he was buried to the hilt. The sensations were powerful. Her position opened her wide for his deep languid thrusts.

He did as she asked. Growing in fervor, his thrusts became wild—hard and deep, causing the air to rush from her lungs as her hips were plowed into the pool table's edge.

Her hands sought something to hold, but the tightly drawn fabric under her had no give. She reached down, seeking the edge of the table, something to hold onto before she shattered into a million pieces.

Sean's weight landed on her from behind. "Put your arms over your head, baby, and keep them there."

His voice was like sandpaper rasping every exposed nerve, his breath moving along the tiny hairs on the back of her neck.

Shaking her head, she said, "I can't, Sean," as she reached back, her body insisting she regain some semblance of control.

When his weight became heavier and she felt his teeth on the back of her neck, she stilled. His large hands firmly grasped her wrists bringing them high above her head, leaving her stretched out beneath him. He was still buried to the hilt inside of her. His warmth could be felt throughout her body, every pulse of his shaft wrenched a shiver from her as she lay pinned beneath him.

"Now keep them right there."

In frustration, she shook her head. Didn't he understand? She needed to be fucked hard and fast. To make it quick so she could get herself back in control. To lose control now while her world felt as if it were falling apart was too dangerous. No good would come of it.

Before she could think any more of such things he began to move. His slow thrusts were making her crazy. Needing more, she lunged back on him causing his penis to delve deep, wringing a groan from him. She felt it vibrate up the back of her neck just before he completely stopped.

Pulling out until just the wide head of his long, thick shaft was lodged at her entrance, he fingered her. Of their own accord, her hips tilted begging for his full length. Sobbing breaths made their way from her pursed lips. If he didn't do something soon she was going to scream.

Pushing herself back against his body, she cried out, "Fuck me already, damn you!"

"Keep your ass still," he said. "If you don't, you may just get more than you bargained for, baby," he added, as his finger played around the entrance of her cock-filled vagina.

Honor shivered with the new sensations coursing through her body. The area Sean was teasing reminded her of the stories she'd heard as a teenager. Later, she'd probably kick herself for asking the question running through her mind but right now she was hot, wet and beyond tipsy.

"You'd never share me would you? I mean with your brothers or anyone else... I've heard stories..." Honor let her words trail off.

Honor wondered briefly if Sean had lost his tongue then she heard him exhale swiftly. "Hell, no!" The words seemed to burst from him as if in anger. "A man doesn't share the woman he loves." Honor said nothing. She merely nodded her head. His words were enough. No sooner had the words left his mouth than the same wicked finger that had been torturing her made its way back up the crease of her bottom until it found her anus spreading her own juices there. It was a threat, a promise. He never said things he didn't mean and always followed through with what he said. Only her drink-sodden mind, along with the little devil riding high on her shoulder, viewed it as a challenge.

A challenge she was more than eager to meet head-on. As his finger slowly circled her virgin entrance, she couldn't help but whimper. The sensations were completely new and so overwhelming she couldn't help but move against him. Her body wiggled and squirmed lodging his shaft deeper into her. His finger continued its journey, collecting moisture from her overflowing sex then spreading it around as his finger teased and tantalized.

Her last thought before her orgasm powered through her was that she was in trouble. Big trouble.

Chapter Twelve

ဢ

After bringing Honor to her pleasure twice without finding his own release, he was beyond ready. He thought about his one main fantasy when it came to making love in his bar and knew he wouldn't take her again as she was, bent over the pool table, although it had been very pleasurable.

He wanted to watch her as he buried himself in her tight ass. God, he hoped like hell she didn't change her mind before he was able to work his way up her tight, dark hole.

Taking a step back, he dislodged himself from her sucking cunt. He then pulled her against his chest. She seemed steady on her feet, but he refused to take her as he planned to without letting her know exactly what she was in for.

And although it would kill him, he would back off if she didn't seem interested or didn't comprehend the magnitude of what it would be like to have every inch of him lodged within her.

"Honor, baby. You with me?"

"Hmm, oh, yeah, but why did you stop? Why are you torturing me, Sean? I want your cock inside me."

To hear her talk so openly, so wantonly, was like music to his ears.

He led her to the bar. Once there, he moved a couple of the stools, leaving just one in front of her.

"I want that, too, Little Darlin', but I want even more."

When she didn't answer, he tilted her head and kissed her long and slow, teasing and tormenting her mouth until she whimpered against his lips.

Pulling ever so slightly away, he told her, "I want to be buried deep inside of you, baby—but I want your ass. I want you on your knees on that stool," he said, motioning to the stool in front of her.

"Then I want those pretty nipples of yours pressed against the bar, your tight little ass in the air, just for me. Just think. Even with you on the stool, I'm still tall enough to take you here." He was squeezing her ass, spreading her cheeks. Her warm skin was smooth against the palm of his hands.

Her breathing was rapid as was her heartbeat. He could see her pulse as it throbbed through the vein in her neck. It seemed like forever when she finally looked up and nodded, her cheeks flushed.

"No," he said. "Don't nod. I want you to tell me."

"Y-yes," she hissed out on a ragged breath.

"Yes what?" He needed to be sure she knew what she was getting into.

She stepped closer burying her face into his chest. "Yes, I want you to. I...uh... I've never done that before, but I want to. I mean... I want you to."

She hadn't said the words, but it would do. It would have to do because if he waited any longer, he was going to explode.

With his hands on her bare hips, he turned her until she faced away from him. Lifting her easily, he settled her onto the stool.

The small round cushion of the stool allowed no room for her to spread her legs, causing a problem because he wanted her spread wide, able to take everything he could give her and then some.

He pulled another stool close leaving a few inches between it and the one she was already on. Then, he helped her settle one knee upon it.

She was completely open to him. Her back rose and fell rapidly with each breath. It took her a minute, but finally, without looking at him, she eased herself forward until her breasts were crushed to the cool wooden surface of the bar. It must have been cold because she shivered with the contact.

When he was sure she was settled, he came up behind her laying a hand at the base of her spine. She jumped at his touch.

"Relax," he soothed, needing to hear the words just the same as she did. He was horny as hell and seeing her up on the stool at the perfect level for his tall frame made it even worse.

He needed to focus, to stay in control and make her first experience a pleasurable one because there would surely be more to follow, if he had his way.

He stroked his hand down over the curve of her ass until his fingers found her dripping pussy.

Good, she was still wet and ready. Gathering what was left of her release, he lubricated the rosette of her anus, getting her used to his touch.

With each passing stroke, he added more and more pressure until she was pliant enough for him to slip the tip of his finger inside.

She was fire-hot and so very tight. He knew there would be no holding back once he was inside her. Continuing on, he worked on her until he could easily introduce first one finger and then a second, being careful to gauge her reaction.

Her whimpers of pleasure were intermingled with an occasional grimace. Her grunts of surprise and the few curse words she let loose were nothing compared to the way her body pressed back begging for more.

And the best part was that he got to watch it all, every reaction to cross her face, in the big mirror behind the bar.

When she was as ready as she'd ever be, he plunged into her pussy, getting his cock nice and wet. She felt like heaven, and he knew he wouldn't last long once inside the forbidden entrance of her nether hole.

One last swipe of his finger spread her arousal to where it was needed. He then began to slowly work his length into her mysterious channel.

She was virgin tight—her body's grasp around his bulbous head was almost painful. Her gasp as his cockhead finally defeated the ring of muscle protecting her entrance caused him to still.

He gave her a couple of minutes to get used to his size before he began to work his way further into her. He watched her in the mirror as he did so, falling in love with her deeper by the minute.

"All right?" he asked when she tensed against him.

Her head came up meeting his gaze in the mirror. Her eyes were no longer distant or confused as they had been previously. Their blue depths were wide, awed as sensation took over.

She was with him all the way. The alcohol must have taken a backseat to her pleasure.

Looking into the mirror, her eyes trained on his, she nodded her head as she grasped the edge of the bar with white-knuckled hands.

His hips lurched forward, his cock delving deep within her ultra-tight tunnel. He wasn't going to make it. Reaching forward, he found the little protruding nub nestled just above her slit. With his thumb and forefinger, he grasped the bundle of nerves and milked it until she cried out.

Her climax was intense, racking her body with spasms, causing him to gasp. The combination of her muscles clutching his length and her cry of release sent him into orbit. He fought the need to pound into her, instead withdrawing in slow increments as her muscles clenched and unclenched around him.

When he was almost all the way out, with just the flared head of his shaft remaining within her, he thrust home while he continued working her clit, drawing out her orgasm. He could feel his imminent release as his balls drew up tightly against his body and he was lost.

Plunging forward, entering her in one swift thrust, he felt his body's signals as a tingle started at the base of his spine.

Once again buried to the hilt, he stilled and growled as he burst deep within her, filling her body with his seed, just as she filled his heart with love.

* * * * *

Her face flamed just as the rest of her body burned. Never before had she felt anything so powerful. At first, she wasn't sure what to think. She'd heard stories and read about it, but had never experienced it. It should be wrong and in the eyes of most, it probably was, but she couldn't think about that just now because right now, all she could do was feel.

His shaft plunged into her throbbing center as his fingers pulled from her back entrance. The overwhelming sensations scared her. There was no turning from them. They were just there. Taking over every nerve ending, every sense her body had and using it against her.

When she felt the blunt tip of his erection between the cheeks of her backside, she did her best to relax. Internally fighting herself, as well as the embarrassment urging her to stop him.

There was no way she would stop him. Her body craved what his offered. A stretching burn stilled not only her thoughts but also her body. Her breath held and she was sure someone had set fire to her.

Burying her face into her arms, she held on. Sean had stilled behind her and she wanted to ask him to pull out of her, to take away the hurt, but at the same time she was afraid he would do just what she asked.

It was crazy, she was crazy, but while the pressure of his entrance was intense, her body gripped him with determined power as if it would refuse to release him.

Her head swam as colors burst in front of her eyes. She realized she was still holding her breath and relaxed enough to let it slowly escape her lungs. The next breaths she took were slow and steady.

And then he began to move.

She couldn't help but tense against the feel of being invaded. When Sean asked if she was all right, she lifted her head from the bar and sought his gaze in the mirror in front of her, and then nodded.

She held onto the bar so tight her hands felt as if they would end up permanently attached to its wooden surface. If she let go though, she feared she would spiral out of control.

After moving in slow, languid movements for what seemed like hours, he thrust the rest of the way into her.

Seated to the hilt, he felt huge. Filling her completely, leaving not a single inch of her internal flesh untouched.

When his hand reached forward, finding her clit, she thought she would die of pleasure. The look of love shining from his hazel eyes added to the intensity level causing her heart to ache.

Honor had no time to think of what it meant to be taken in such a way by a man like Sean O'Malley. She didn't have time to realize that there would never be another man in her life, in her bed, because a forceful sensation started tingling throughout her body.

"Oh, oh, shit!" she gasped. "Ohmygod, ohmygod…yes!" It came out part hiss, part scream as her body erupted. Sean had brought her to many mind-numbing orgasms, but this— this was so much more in so many ways.

She had no control over her body. Her back arched pulling him deeper into her. He was so big that she could feel every inch of him, every vein and ridge of his throbbing shaft as it remained buried deep inside of her.

She could feel him slowly pulling out of her body. It clutched and grasped in response. His movement stopped with just the tip of him still inside her. That part of him was broader than the rest causing a slight burn in the muscles surrounding her entrance.

His look was intimidating as she watched in the mirror. His eyes were hooded, his lids lowered until she almost couldn't see the color of his irises.

Sweat beaded on his bald head, his hands grasped her hips tightly. Something flashed across his face an instant before he lunged into her causing the air to be forced from her lungs.

His body stilled against hers, a growl erupting from deep within his broad muscled chest, then she felt the warmth as his semen filled her.

His penis throbbed and jerked with its release sending her over the edge and back into oblivion. Her plea for mercy rent the air just as he leaned forward wrapping one arm around her waist, his head a heavy weight on her back.

When he finally moved, she groaned. She didn't want him to leave her, but knew he must if she ever planned to walk straight again. That thought brought a smile to her mouth.

Her smile completely faded as he pulled from her body. A gasp found its way through her lips before she could hold it back.

"You okay, Little Darlin'?" he asked, genuine concern in his voice.

Honor nodded. She was sore, but in a good way. Now she just needed to figure out how in the world to look the man in the eye after she'd just had anal sex over a bar with him. Her whole body was probably blushing at the thought.

When she turned to leave, wanting to find her clothes, he snagged her arm.

"Not again!" he thundered. "I won't let you shut me out again, Honor. Now get your clothes on. We're going home and in the morning we are going to talk."

Her eyes narrowed to slits at his retreating back. It was then that she realized he had never even removed his clothes. She covered her face and groaned.

Praying for patience with the overbearing man who believed he loved her, she dressed and waited until he came back into the room. Then without so much as a word, she was herded to his vehicle and driven to his house.

As they reached his house, she idly wondered if she should lay into him now or save it for tomorrow when she was rested.

Chapter Thirteen
ಐ

He fought the need to shake her. She'd tried to slip out of his grasp again and he just wouldn't allow it. In order to retain what was left of his composure, Sean kept quiet on the drive home.

She was glaring blue daggers in his direction — it was actually a bit amusing. He wondered if she would do something to warrant another spanking before the night was over. He certainly hoped so.

Sean watched the road, but out the corner of his eye, he watched as Honor sat stiffly beside him staring out the side window.

She might be stubborn but he was determined, and there was no way in hell he was letting her out of his sight before he knew just what was bothering her.

Once that was finished, he would insist that she stay with him, for good, as his wife. And if she refused…well…he didn't want to think about that.

When he had her safely in his home, he turned to her. The weary look in her eyes and the slouch of her shoulders spoke of her inner turmoil, as well as the exhaustion her body felt.

He wanted to know, but wasn't willing to push — at least not tonight. "Come on, sweetheart."

He grasped her hand, tugging her along behind him. In his room, the door securely closed, he began to undress her. Removing first her snug-fitting blouse and then the drawstring pants she seemed to favor.

"Sean?" she questioned.

He could see the hesitancy in her eyes and smiled a crooked smile in return. "Just to sleep, Honor. I just want to hold you next to me while you sleep."

She seemed to melt within his arms. Her body relaxed instantly at his words. He couldn't quite figure out if that was a good thing or not.

Once he had peeled every garment from her body, he scooped her into his arms, holding her close to his heart for the briefest of moments before laying her on the bed.

He imagined the clean cotton sheets felt cool against her skin and hastily discarded his clothes to join her. Pulling her close to his body in spoon fashion, her back to his front, they quickly drifted off to sleep.

It seemed as though he had only been asleep for a few minutes when something woke him. Honor was no longer in his arms, or even close to him. Her thrashing body was completely on the other side of his king-sized bed.

She was struggling against an unknown force calling out as if in pain. Her keening moan sent shivers down his spine. Tears were streaming down her face even as her eyes stayed tightly closed. It tore at his heart to see her this way.

Whatever was bothering her was taking an emotional toll on her.

She'd had many restless nights recently and even a few bad dreams she'd insisted she didn't remember, but nothing of this extent. The thought that she'd been suffering alone or didn't trust him enough to tell him what was wrong drove Sean crazy.

No wonder she looked tired and had been short-tempered and restless.

Just then, she let out an ear-piercing scream. "Nooo! Oh, God, please!" she sobbed in her sleep.

Sean pulled her into his arms needing to feel her soft, warm flesh against his. "Honor," he called to her. When she didn't answer, only thrashed in his arms fighting his hold, his tone became more firm. "Honor! Darlin', wake up. Please, baby. Wake up." The last came out a ragged whispered plea.

Her body stilled, her lids fluttering for a second before they opened. He could see her confusion as she gazed up at him. It only lasted a moment before she buried her face into the crook of his neck and broke down.

Her whole body shook uncontrollably. Her sobbing breaths filled the air and made him want to kill whoever had hurt her. He couldn't imagine what she'd been through to cause so much pain but if there were anything he could do to make it better, it would be done.

"Honor? Tell me what it is. Let me help," he pleaded with her.

She lifted her head the slightest bit as she tried to regain her composure but it was no use.

"Please, baby. Don't cry. Oh, God, Honor. Please tell me." He could no longer hide his own misery. His chest ached with it. To see the woman who was a part of him suffering left him in doubt of his strength.

What if he couldn't handle what she told him? What would he do if her secret was so horrible that he could not deal with it?

* * * * *

His chest felt so good against her as her body fought the memories the dreams always seemed to force on her. No longer would she be able to hold back the truth and she knew it.

When the disturbing images faded, Honor lifted her head and dried her eyes. There was nothing easy about it, but it had to be done.

She sat back until she was no longer enveloped within the warmth of Sean's arms and then she sought out his face.

His eyes were tortured and red as if he himself had been experiencing her pain.

Was it possible to care so deeply for someone that you could feel what they felt? It was, and with that startling realization, Honor knew beyond the shadow of a doubt that she was deeply, irreversibly in love with Sean O'Malley, and she cursed a silent blue streak for allowing it to happen.

Squaring her shoulders, she looked him in the eye and began. She told him everything from how she had oohed and aahed over the new car, bothering her parents daily about it, to how she had felt when the police had showed up at her door to break the news of the accident. She cried through an explanation about how, as a teenager, she had personally blamed herself and how that even now she sometimes couldn't help but wonder if things would be different had she not begged with every breath for a car.

Before she had finished, she'd broken eye contact. She just couldn't stand to see the pity on his face as he gazed back at her.

When the bed dipped then immediately sprang back after releasing his weight, her heart dropped. Willing herself to stay strong only lasted until she heard the soft click of a door closing. It was as she had thought, and she hated herself for not telling him earlier.

If only she had been able to keep her heart locked tightly away, then she could have avoided the misery she was feeling. Her shoulders shook, but this time she grieved quietly.

So caught up in the torment coursing through her, Honor didn't hear when Sean opened the door and made his way into the room.

It wasn't until the mattress once again dipped with the extra weight that she lifted her head, prepared for the worst only to feel the warm moisture of a washcloth make its way over her face.

"I'm so sorry, Little Darlin'. You shouldn't have had to go through all of that. I didn't know it at the time you came to live in Texas with your aunt." His eyes were suspiciously bright as he held her chin giving him better access to her tear-stained face.

He continued with his gentle cleansing as he spoke. "Never doubt for a minute that your parents loved you just as you love them. It doesn't end when they're gone, baby, just as my love for you will never end. Nothing about the accident was your fault, Honor. It was an accident and if I have to, I'll remind you of that fact daily."

"I know they loved me, Sean. This time of year is just so hard and even though I know better, I feel as though I have to find a way to forgive myself all over again."

Sean looked at her, his hazel eyes filled with emotion. "There is nothing to forgive, Honor. You were a child excited about a gift. What happened was not your fault." His voice was rough, yet stern.

"I don't know what to think anymore, Sean. I just don't know." Honor's voice broke and once again, tears streamed down her face. "I do so good all year but I didn't realize just how alone I was until my aunt died and I came back to Texas."

Sean's arms closed around her, tight and comforting. "You don't have to know, Little Darlin', you just have to let go. It's not going to come easy but it will come, and just in case you've got doubts, I'll be right here to make sure you see it happen. You're not in this alone, Honor. You'll never be alone again."

"That's what I'm afraid of."

Sean looked at her as if he was trying to figure out what she meant. The question in his eyes prodded her on.

"I've never let myself love, Sean. I'm not so sure I could survive such a loss again."

"Oh, Darlin'," Sean murmured, gathering her in his arms. "We can't choose who we love, it just happens. I can't change the way I feel about you, Honor, and I won't even try. To do so would be a disservice to the both of us."

This time she looked into his hazel eyes, really looked. They were bright with his love, gold flecks intermingled within their depths and she knew she was home. No more wandering. No more hiding, she'd finally made it. She was exactly where she belonged.

With a nod of her head, she moved forward placing a tender kiss upon his lips. Backing away, she stared into his eyes. "I love you, Sean O'Malley, with all my heart. Will you marry me?"

His big body tensed, a wide smile crossed his face as a lone tear trickled down his cheek.

"I never thought you'd ask, Little Darlin'," he gruffly answered, kissing her until she thought she'd collapse from sheer excitement and lack of air.

He then proceeded to show her just how much he truly loved her. Very slowly, and long into the night, until they finally drifted off to sleep just before dawn.

Chapter Fourteen

క౧

The next few days were extremely hectic, but they had made it through Honor's birthday, just the two of them. The day had been spent loving each other and talking.

It had taken some coaxing, but he'd managed to get her to share some of the good memories she'd kept deeply buried. They'd laughed and cried, and beyond all that, they'd loved, over and over until they lay, bodies sated within the twisted and tangled sheets of the bed.

With a proud pitch to his voice, Sean announced their news to Zane and Hayden. Both were ecstatic as was Zane's fiancée Serena. There was already talk of a double wedding.

Sean wasn't sure he was willing to wait that long, but once he saw the look on Honor's face, he bit his tongue. If it would make her happy, he'd do it.

Several times during the past week, Serena had been by to visit with Honor. It was nice to see the two of them together.

He'd even managed to make a trip with her to meet his father. Zane and Serena had gone along with them. It was a tense few minutes early on in the meeting, but things had really changed with the old man.

It still seemed strange. It had been an ongoing battle since as far back as he could remember. His father, Colin O'Malley, had wanted his sons to follow in his footsteps, and as a result of his persistence, had pretty much alienated all three of them. During the normal course of things Sean and his brothers would go to their father's for Christmas supper, but other than that, the occasional phone call was all that passed between them.

It really was a shame, but after the last meeting, Sean was in hopes that all of that would change. As a matter of fact, he was almost sure it would. The look on his father's face when Honor and Serena had asked him to give them away had been one of surprise. Joy had quickly taken over and before the four of them left, laughter had filled the room.

It was amazing what love could conquer.

It was Friday night. Sean frowned when Hayden walked into the bar with a scowl plastered across his face. His mood was surly at best, and Sean could imagine just who had put him in such a mood.

He'd bet a free round for the bar that a short woman with sparkling green eyes had something to do with it. *This could be fun*, he thought, as Hayden stomped to the bar and parked himself on a stool.

"Beer?" Sean asked.

"Hell, no," his brother replied. "Whiskey, make it a double." He looked as if he were ready to commit murder.

"Problem?" He was doing his best not to laugh, but it was getting harder by the minute.

"None of your damned business!" Hayden growled at him, throwing back the glass of whiskey in one fell swoop.

Sean studied his brother for a split second before deciding that there really was something bothering him.

"Aw, hell, Hayden, it can't be that bad," he said, trying to lighten the mood. Instead, he received a narrowed look.

"That damned woman is going to be the death of me. She's driving me crazy and I can't even fire her. How's that for stuck?"

Hayden seemed truly flustered and Sean couldn't stop from asking.

"What did Austin do this time?" He knew it was Austin because there wasn't another soul on earth who would dare push Hayden to the point of heavy drinking and get away with it.

Pouring his brother another drink, he crossed his arms over the bulk of his chest and waited. It didn't take long.

"She's doing another one of those damned parties tonight. I told her I didn't like her doing it, but do you think she'd listen?"

Without waiting for a reply, he continued on with his tirade. "Hell, no! She told me I had no say in what she did after hours. The thing that really chaps my ass is that she's right. God dammit! I'd like to throttle the brat with my bare hands."

Sean hadn't heard much past the point where Hayden said Austin was hosting a party tonight.

"Did you say Austin's party was tonight?"

Hayden pinned him with a dark look. "As if you didn't know," he snarled.

"How in the hell would I know? And when is the party because Austin was supposed to be getting together with Honor and Serena tonight? That's why Honor isn't here."

With another look from Hayden, Sean wiped his brow and cursed. "Oh, hell, no." He pulled the apron from his waist and strode around the bar. *Thank God, I have trustworthy employees,* he thought as he hollered over his shoulder that he was leaving and wouldn't be back to close. He'd end up paying some overtime but it would be worth every single cent.

"Where?" was the single worded question. Sean was afraid he knew the answer even as he asked the question. Every hair on the back of his neck stood at attention. If his hunch was right, Honor, Serena and Austin were holed up at his place with a bunch of giggling women with dildos. Sean didn't have time to think on it much before Hayden started bitching again.

"How in the hell should I know? Austin slammed the door in my face before I could ask."

Sean wanted to laugh at Hayden's disgruntled voice. Hell, he couldn't care less if Honor wanted to go to one of those adult-toy parties, but he'd be damned if she was going to get away with sneaking it by him.

It was Austin The Hellion he didn't trust. No telling what that woman would talk Honor into doing or buying.

Come to think of it, the buying part wasn't too bad as long as he got to use them on her, with her. It might not all be bad, but he was certainly going to enjoy laying into her ass. There would be no sneaking behind his back and she'd learn it soon enough.

Just as they rounded the last table, the front door opened and in walked Zane.

"Just in time, little brother."

"Where are you two going in such a hurry?" Zane asked, a puzzled look on his face.

"Us three, you mean. You're involved too," Hayden answered.

Before Zane could say another word, Sean added, "Just come on. We'll tell you on the way."

He wanted to get going. His palms were tingling in anticipation. His cock was already half-hard and would be uncomfortably engorged before they even got there if he didn't change his train of thought.

Once they were all settled in the spacious interior of Hayden's pickup, Sean told all. A wide, wicked-looking grin stole across Zane's face as he rubbed his hands together.

Sean couldn't help but chuckle. If the look on Zane's face was any indication, Serena had also overlooked telling Zane exactly where she would be and what she'd be doing.

"So," Sean said. "I take it you didn't know what was going on either?"

"Nope, seems Serena left a few things out." His grin just about split his face now.

Sean couldn't help but feel a bit sorry for Serena. It seemed she was going to be in big trouble when Zane got a hold of her. He'd wondered since Zane's return to Texas, but now he was almost sure. Zane and Serena had a special type of relationship, one he could almost bet bordered on kinky as hell.

That thought alone was enough to bring his half-hard shaft to full-blown hard-as-a-rock. Now to hunt down the prize.

* * * * *

Honor couldn't believe they'd gotten away with it, for now at least. Austin had planned it just right. It seemed that between Serena and Austin, she had some friends. It was a good feeling.

The room of women laughed at something Austin said. The woman really was a riot. The three of them, as well as several other local women Austin invited, had spent the last two hours talking about everything imaginable.

The assortment of adult toys sitting on every smooth surface of Sean's living room kept the conversation as well as the laughter going.

Honor wondered when it would all finally erupt. She was betting that they didn't have long before the O'Malley brothers would break up their little get-together.

She and Serena were looking forward to it. They both agreed there was just something about the rough and gruff O'Malley men that kept a woman in wet panties.

Little tremors made their way stealthily through her core even as her bottom quivered in expectancy. She'd have to do her best to act surprised as well as affronted by the fact that the men thought they could dictate where they were and who they were with.

After all, it would do no good to get herself so worked up that she threw herself over Sean's lap begging to be spanked.

A small giggle escaped at the thought. Nervous anticipation made its way through her body.

Serena, who kept checking her watch, must be feeling the same erotic sensations. For some reason, Honor couldn't help but wonder if they'd gone overboard just a bit. The way Serena's fingers slightly trembled as she fingered the wide gold choker made Honor think that the other woman's punishment might be a bit more severe than her own.

She wasn't worried though, because Serena's eyes were aglow. Her head kept cocking to the side as if she were listening for something. Nope, Serena was just as sexually excited as Honor was herself.

Austin was the one who was confusing her. The woman seemed to be preparing for a battle. She had denied until she was blue in the face the possibility of having feelings for Hayden. It didn't matter to Honor what she insisted, you could see it plainly written across her face every time she looked at the rugged rancher.

Her eagerness for the fight ahead showed in every nuance of her face. Her chin was held just a bit higher than usual. Her green eyes glittered with attitude. It was going to be one hell of a night.

The front door flew open, banging into the wall behind it. Austin winked at Honor and Serena as she mumbled beneath her breath, "Let the games begin."

Three large men stood in the doorway, only moving as the room at large quieted. Within seconds, the women in the room not directly associated with the three excused themselves and beat a hasty retreat.

Sean walked up to where she sat, grabbed her gently, but firmly by the upper arms and pulled her to her feet. It took everything she had not to let loose with the smile trying to cross her face.

"Hey, honey. What are you doing home already?" she asked with all the innocence she could muster. It was an extremely hard thing to do, considering the biggest dildo she'd ever seen was standing straight up on the cabinet just behind him.

His eyes narrowed as he studied her face. They glittered in warning. A warning she once again decided to ignore. But before she was able to push further, Austin spoke up.

"Son of a bitch, Sean. Ya couldn't wait 'til the party was over? Those women you just scared off seemed real interested in ordering some of my stuff." She motioned around the room, bringing attention to the assortment of toys.

Honor watched in morbid fascination as his eyes widened and his face turned beet red. The color rode high on his cheeks, his pupils dilated, just before his hand ran down the length of her back until it met the swell of her backside.

Her breath hissed from between her lips as his hand contracted, squeezing her cheek. She wanted to shout for joy, to crow in triumph. Instead, she met his gaze and gave just the slightest struggle. As she knew it would, her movement sent him into Neanderthal mode, causing him to pull her closer, tightening his hold.

She could feel the length of his arousal as it pressed against her. The sensation opened the floodgates. Honor wondered if she would ever have the privilege of wearing dry panties again.

Swiveling her head, she found Serena. The woman was being held tightly in front of Zane, her back to his chest. A look of utter contentment was plastered across her face.

Through the silky fabric of her shirt, Honor could see Serena's peaked nipples. A shiver ran through the other woman's body as Zane leaned in and whispered something into her ear.

Without a word, Serena turned and left the room. Zane eyed Honor and Austin before he nodded to his brothers. Just before leaving the room, he snatched a red leather flogger from the coffee table.

Pinning Austin with a look, he said, "You can collect for this later."

He then left the room looking like a man on a mission. The look of promised retribution on his face fanned Honor's arousal to a flaming inferno.

When she squirmed against Sean's body, he clamped her against him in an iron-tight hold. "Don't," he growled, not caring if Austin and Hayden heard.

Honor shook her head when Austin moved to step forward. It would do no good to get the tiny woman deeper into her scheme. She was just opening her mouth to apologize for Sean's behavior when she was interrupted.

"Hayden, why don't you see what you can do with her?" Sean said, nodding toward Austin. Then in a low voice that vibrated along the surface of her skin, he added, "And I'll take care of this one."

Chapter Fifteen

80

Sean couldn't help but smile as Honor began to struggle in earnest. That little dance she'd been doing before was all for show. He'd known it just as soon as it had started.

Could see in her eyes just how much she loved the whole ordeal.

Her wide, blue eyes had taken in the whole thing. Every detail of how Zane and Serena had interacted with each other. He would have to admit, their relationship fascinated him as well.

Hayden was still watching Austin as if she might try to flee the room. He was poised and ready to pounce. He idly wondered how Hayden would take care of the hoyden. After all, his brother had no claim on her. At least none he was willing to admit to.

Right now though, that wasn't his problem. His problem was arching her back against his hold and fighting like a wildcat.

He let the depth of his lust show as one corner of his mouth lifted. Staring her in the eye, he wondered curiously exactly when she noticed he was for real.

"Sean O'Malley, you had better put me down!"

God, she was beautiful all ruffled and red. "Soon, Darlin'. Real soon."

He wanted to march her up the hall and into their bedroom to meet her fate, but his curiosity got the best of him so he decided to wait and see what Hayden would do.

"Pack up your goodies, brat," Hayden said to Austin, leaning against the door in what may have seemed like a casual pose to a bystander, but Sean knew better.

Sean watched as Austin crossed her arms under her breasts causing them to swell until she almost flowed over the top of her tiny blouse.

The woman really did have a very impressive set on her, and he wasn't the only one to notice because Hayden's eyes had definitely traveled south.

"It's after hours, Hayden. You have no say in what I do, dammit! So remember that the next time you go gettin' all high and mighty." She kept spewing venom as her anger grew — all the while, she packed her bags, preparing to leave.

When she was done, she turned to Honor and said, "See ya soon, sweetie." The wink aimed at him took Sean by surprise. The three musketeers must have been in cahoots.

Hayden stepped forward with the intention of grabbing one of her duffel bags, but jerked his hand back when Austin smacked it.

"Get your damned hands off my stuff, ya big ass. You gave up all right to touch me or my stuff, so don't you forget it."

Sean couldn't help but wonder at the hurt tone of Austin's voice. He knew good and well that Hayden was attracted to her, and couldn't imagine for the life of him why his brother refused to act on that attraction, but he wasn't about to get into the middle of it. Right now, he had his own brat to deal with.

The only thing he heard as Hayden moved closer to Austin was, "The hell I did." The ominous words were low and dangerous, and Sean was extremely grateful they weren't aimed at him.

Evidently, Austin Calhoun didn't know better than to go toe-to-toe with Hayden when he was struck by a black mood.

Sean figured that by the time the night was over, she'd never forget the lesson.

The soft click of the door set him in motion. Dragging a struggling Honor, he made his way to their room where he'd have all night long to show her just how much he loved her.

* * * * *

Honor shrieked as she was lifted and dropped unceremoniously onto the bed. All around her objects bounced as her body weight continued to disturb the mattress.

"Oh, hell," she muttered, when she finally realized what she was seeing. Peeking way up into Sean's face, she watched as his eyes took in what had just been flung from the box that was now setting on the floor beside the bed.

Honor didn't realize until just that moment exactly how much of Austin's merchandise she'd bought. She could feel the flush as it stole its way up her neck and face.

Grabbing a medium-sized vibrator, Sean ground out through gritted teeth, "Have you used any of this stuff?"

His tone made her wary. She couldn't catch her breath much less enough air for words, so she shook her head.

"Little Darlin', I don't mind toys, but if you use them while I'm home, I'll paddle your ass. Do you understand?"

Oh, yeah, she understood perfectly. As a matter of fact, she was making notes so she'd know exactly what to do the next time she needed a good spanking.

She nodded her head.

"If anything makes its way up that tight little pussy of yours, I'll be the one putting it there. If I'm to be gone for some reason, I'll supply the batteries." He chuckled when her face flushed even further.

"Now undress." It was a gruff command, issued as he began undressing himself.

Honor couldn't help but scramble to her feet. Her fingers weren't cooperating so it took longer to remove her clothes than she'd have liked.

When she was completely nude, Sean strode across the room. He flicked the switch, plunging the room into darkness. She could see nothing. The sensation heightened her other senses allowing her to hear his every move as he made his way across the thick, carpeted floor.

In the next instant, there was an amber glow flowing across the room. A single candle burned on the chest of drawers directly across from her.

The look in Sean's eyes was just as hot, just as glowing. Possessive and feral in its intent, causing mini-spasms to rack the tiny internal muscles of her vagina. His hooded gaze made promises Honor's body instantly recognized.

As he made his way to her, she couldn't help the overabundance of love swelling within her chest. From that moment on, the rest of their night was inundated with peaks and valleys. Over and over again, they soared through raging infernos only to swoop back down through the blissful valleys. When she was completely and utterly sated, she curled herself into the warm wall of flesh beside her, knowing full well she would spend the rest of her life honoring Sean.

Why an electronic book?

We live in the Information Age—an exciting time in the history of human civilization, in which technology rules supreme and continues to progress in leaps and bounds every minute of every day. For a multitude of reasons, more and more avid literary fans are opting to purchase e-books instead of paper books. The question from those not yet initiated into the world of electronic reading is simply: *Why?*

1. *Price.* An electronic title at Ellora's Cave Publishing and Cerridwen Press runs anywhere from 40% to 75% less than the cover price of the exact same title in paperback format. Why? Basic mathematics and cost. It is less expensive to publish an e-book (no paper and printing, no warehousing and shipping) than it is to publish a paperback, so the savings are passed along to the consumer.

2. *Space.* Running out of room in your house for your books? That is one worry you will never have with electronic books. For a low one-time cost, you can purchase a handheld device specifically designed for e-reading. Many e-readers have large, convenient screens for viewing. Better yet, hundreds of titles can be stored within your new library—on a single microchip. There are a variety of e-readers from different manufacturers. You can also read e-books on your PC or laptop computer. (Please note that Ellora's Cave does not endorse any specific brands.

You can check our websites at www.ellorascave.com or www.cerridwenpress.com for information we make available to new consumers.)

3. *Mobility.* Because your new e-library consists of only a microchip within a small, easily transportable e-reader, your entire cache of books can be taken with you wherever you go.

4. *Personal Viewing Preferences.* Are the words you are currently reading too small? Too large? Too… ANNOYING? Paperback books cannot be modified according to personal preferences, but e-books can.

5. *Instant Gratification.* Is it the middle of the night and all the bookstores near you are closed? Are you tired of waiting days, sometimes weeks, for bookstores to ship the novels you bought? Ellora's Cave Publishing sells instantaneous downloads twenty-four hours a day, seven days a week, every day of the year. Our webstore is never closed. Our e-book delivery system is 100% automated, meaning your order is filled as soon as you pay for it.

Those are a few of the top reasons why electronic books are replacing paperbacks for many avid readers.

As always, Ellora's Cave and Cerridwen Press welcome your questions and comments. We invite you to email us at Comments@ellorascave.com or write to us directly at Ellora's Cave Publishing Inc., 1056 Home Avenue, Akron, OH 44310-3502.

COMING TO A BOOKSTORE NEAR YOU!

ELLORA'S CAVE

Bestselling Authors Tour

UPDATES AVAILABLE AT

WWW.ELLORASCAVE.COM

erridwen, the Celtic Goddess of wisdom, was the muse who brought inspiration to storytellers and those in the creative arts. Cerridwen Press encompasses the best and most innovative stories in all genres of today's fiction. Visit our site and discover the newest titles by talented authors who still get inspired - much like the ancient storytellers did, once upon a time.

Discover for yourself why readers can't get enough
of the multiple award-winning publisher
Ellora's Cave.

Whether you prefer e-books or paperbacks,

be sure to visit EC on the web at
www.ellorascave.com

for an erotic reading experience that will leave you
breathless.

Made in the USA